"I'm not in th
so if there's son

A figure, blurred by the sunlight, stepped through the door from the adjoining room.

"Hello, Sage," a husky male voice said.

She knew that voice. It haunted her dreams.

"No," she said, while her heart tried to claw its way out of her throat.

"How nice to see you again."

"No," she repeated, the word a papery whisper.

She stumbled back as the figure moved away from the light and became a man.

Tall. Broad-shouldered. Lean.

"Caleb?" she whispered.

His smile was cold and cruel, and it transformed his beautiful face into a dangerous mask.

"Smart girl," he said.

THE WILDE BROTHERS

Wilde by name, unashamedly wild by nature!

They work hard, but you can be damned sure they play even harder! For as long as any of them could remember, they've always loved the same things: Danger…and beautiful women.

They gladly took up the call to serve their country, but duty, honour and pride are words that mask the scars of a true warrior. Now, one by one, the brothers return to their family ranch in Texas.

Can their hearts be tamed in the place they once called home?

Meet the deliciously sexy **Wilde Brothers** in this sizzling and utterly unmissable new family dynasty by much-loved author Sandra Marton!

In August you met

THE DANGEROUS JACOB WILDE

Dare you try to resist

THE RUTHLESS CALEB WILDE

this month?

Look out for Travis's story in 2013!

THE RUTHLESS
CALEB WILDE

BY
SANDRA MARTON

MILLS & BOON

First published in Great Britain 2012
by Mills & Boon, an imprint of Harlequin (UK) Limited.
Harlequin (UK) Limited, Eton House, 18-24 Paradise Road,
Richmond, Surrey TW9 1SR

© Sandra Marton 2012

ISBN: 978 0 263 89142 3

Harlequin (UK) policy is to use papers that are natural, renewable and recyclable products and made from wood grown in sustainable forests. The logging and manufacturing process conform to the legal environmental regulations of the country of origin.

Printed and bound in Spain
by Blackprint CPI, Barcelona

Sandra Marton wrote her first novel while she was still in primary school. Her doting parents told her she'd be a writer some day, and Sandra believed them. In secondary school and college she wrote dark poetry nobody but her boyfriend understood—though, looking back, she suspects he was just being kind. As a wife and mother she wrote murky short stories in what little spare time she could manage, but not even her boyfriend-turned-husband could pretend to understand those. Sandra tried her hand at other things, among them teaching and serving on the Board of Education in her home town, but the dream of becoming a writer was always in her heart.

At last Sandra realised she wanted to write books about what all women hope to find: love with that one special man, love that's rich with fire and passion, love that lasts for ever. She wrote a novel, her very first, and sold it to Mills & Boon® Modern™ Romance. Since then she's written more than sixty books, all of them featuring sexy, gorgeous, larger-than-life heroes. A four-time RITA® award finalist, she's also received five *RT Book Reviews* magazine awards, and has been honoured with *RT*'s Career Achievement Award for Series Romance. Sandra lives with her very own sexy, gorgeous, larger-than-life hero in a sun-filled house on a quiet country lane in the north-eastern United States.

Recent titles by the same author:

Did you know these are also available as eBooks?
Visit www.millsandboon.co.uk

CHAPTER ONE

CALEB Wilde was doing his best to look like a man having a good time.

No question, he should have been.

He was in New York, one of his favorite cities, at a party in a SoHo club so trendy that the entrance door was unmarked.

Not that *trendy* was the description he'd have chosen.

Pretentious struck him as closer to the truth, but hey, what did he know?

Caleb smothered a yawn.

His brain had gone on holiday.

Not because of the noise, even though the sound level in the enormous room was somewhere in the stratosphere, but what else would it be when the DJ was so famous he signed autographs between sets?

Not because of the booze, either. Caleb had been nursing the same tumbler of Scotch almost the entire evening.

And it was definitely not because the party was dull.

The client he'd flown in to see was throwing it to celebrate his fortieth birthday. The room was packed with Names. Hedge-fund managers. International bankers. Media moguls. Hollywood glitterati. European royals. Second-tier, but royals just the same.

And, of course, the requisite scores of stunning women.

The problem was, Caleb was too tired to appreciate any of it.

He'd been on the go since before dawn. A 7:00 a.m. meeting with a client in his Dallas office. A 10:00 a.m. meeting with his brothers at the Wilde ranch. The flight to New York on one of the family's private jets. Late lunch with this client, the birthday boy. Drinks and dinner with an old pal from his shadowy days working for The Agency.

Caleb smothered another yawn.

Tired didn't come close. He was damned near out on his feet, and only courtesy had brought him here tonight.

Well, courtesy and curiosity.

He'd celebrated his own birthday not very long ago. A barbecue at the ranch with his brothers and his new sister-in-law, phone calls from his sisters, one from the General—it came two days late, but hey, when you had a world to run, you were always busy.

Everything had been fun, relaxed and low-key. Nothing like this.

"This guy is a little long in the tooth for trendy clubs," Caleb had told his brothers this morning.

"Because," Travis had said solemnly, "you certainly are."

"Well, yeah. I mean, no, not exactly. I mean—"

"We know what you mean," Jacob had said as solemnly as Travis. "You're a dinosaur."

"Absolutely. We can hear your bones creak."

His brothers had exchanged looks. Then they'd started to laugh.

"You guys sound like a pair of chickens," Caleb had said with what he hoped sounded like indignation.

"Cluck-cluck," Jake had cackled, and that had done it. The three of them had grinned, done the obligatory elbow-in-the-ribs, high-five thing grown men do when they love each other, and Caleb, on an exaggerated sigh had said, yeah, okay, he'd make the sacrifice and go to the party.

"And report back," Travis had added, waggling his eyebrows. "'Cause we equally ancient wise ones want all the details."

Caleb lifted the Scotch to his lips now and sipped at it.

So far, the details were just what he'd expected.

From the balcony, where he'd settled once he'd found his host and engaged in the necessary two minutes of shouted conversation, he had a view of everything happening on the dance floor. It was crowded up here but nothing compared to the situation down below.

The DJ high up on a platform. The pulsing lights. What looked like a thousand sweaty bodies gyrating in their glow.

And the women, all of them spectacular, lots of them interested enough to give him smiles and glances that only a dead man wouldn't be able to interpret.

No big surprise there.

It wasn't his doing, it was the Wilde DNA, a mix of Roman centurion and Viking blood tempered by more than a touch of what was probably Comanche or Kiowa.

The Wilde sisters teased him and his brothers about their looks, and showed no mercy.

"Oh, oh, oh," Jaimie would say, in a perfect imitation of a swooning Victorian maiden.

"Be still, my heart," Emily would sigh, her hand plastered to the center of her chest.

"So tall. So dark. So dangerous," was Lissa's line, delivered with all the drama of an old-time movie star.

And this was perfect Wilde territory. So many beautiful women...

Except, tonight, Caleb wasn't interested.

"Ah'm jest a country boy from Tex-ass," he'd told the blonde who'd slithered over a little while ago.

That had gotten rid of her, fast.

Actually, he'd been pretty hard on her, but then, what kind of female batted her lashes at a man and asked, in a breathy little voice he figured was supposed to be cute, was he somebody rich and famous that she was supposed to recognize?

In truth, he was. Rich, for sure. Famous, too, in corporate and legal circles.

Her approach was at least honest.

It certainly was different.

Another time, he might have smiled and said he was both, and what did she intend to do about it?

Not tonight.

Right now, he thought, glancing at his watch, what he wanted was for another thirty, thirty-five minutes to slip past. Then he could find his host, if that was possible, tell him he'd had a great time and he was sorry as hell but he had an early-morning appointment back in Dallas...

"...for you?"

Caleb turned around. There was a girl standing just in back of him. Pretty, not spectacular, not in a crowd like this but still, she was pretty. Tall. Blonde. Big blue eyes.

Lots of makeup.

Too much for his tastes. Not that his tastes mattered.

Pretty or not, he wasn't in the mood.

"Sorry," he said, "but I'm going to leave soon."

She leaned in a little. Her breasts brushed lightly against his arm and she pulled back but the contact, quick as it was, shot straight through him.

She spoke again. He still couldn't hear her, thanks to the music, but he could certainly take a second look.

What the hell was that thing she was wearing? A dress, or something that could have been a dress if you'd added another twelve inches of fabric. It was black. Or deep blue. Iridescent, anyway, glittery, or maybe it was the effect of the light.

Either way, the dress looked as if it had been glued on her. Skinny straps. Low bodice. A sinfully low bodice, revealing the curve of lush breasts.

His gaze drifted lower, to where the dress ended at the very tops of her thighs.

To his amazement, he felt his body and brain coming back on-line.

He smiled. The girl didn't.

"I'm Caleb," he said. "I didn't get your name."

Those big blue eyes turned icy.

"I didn't give it."

So much for that. She might be in the mood for games. He sure as hell wasn't.

"In that case," he said in his best, intimidate-the-witness tone, "why are you talking to me?"

"I'm paid to talk to you," she said, her voice as cold as her eyes.

"Well, that's certainly blunt but I promise you, lady, I am absolutely not inter—"

"I'm paid to ask what you're drinking. And to bring you a refill." This time, the look she gave him was filled with stony satisfaction. "I'm a waitress, *sir*. Trust me. I wouldn't have looked at you twice if I weren't."

Caleb blinked.

Over the years, a couple of women had told him off. There was the girl in fifth grade, Carrie or Corey, something like that, who'd slugged him after he'd made fun of her over some silly thing at recess. And a mistress—a former mistress— who'd told him exactly what he could do with the farewell sapphire earrings he'd sent her after she'd told him it was time they set a wedding date.

Neither had put him in his place better than this, or even as well.

He supposed he ought to be angry.

He wasn't.

The fact was, he admired Blondie's gumption. An old-fashioned, down-home word, *gumption,* but it was eminently suitable.

That face, that body, that dress…she'd probably been hit on a dozen times tonight until she'd finally thought, *enough!*

He wasn't foolish enough to think she could have avoided the problem by wearing something else.

Caleb had worked his way through law school, rather than touch his father's money or the money he'd inherited from his mother.

He'd delivered pizza, waited tables at Friendly's, worked at an off-campus bar.

There'd been a dress code for the wait staff at the bar.

For the men: white shirts, black bow ties, black trousers, black shoes.

For the women: black ribbons around their throats, low-cut white T-shirts a size too small, swingy black skirts that barely covered their asses and black stiletto heels.

Or they were fired.

Sexual discrimination was alive and well in twenty-first century America. As a lawyer, as a man, Caleb knew that.

Still, he figured he deserved better than being treated like some kind of predator.

He told that to Blondie.

She raised her chin.

"Is that a 'no' to another drink?" she said coldly.

"That's exactly what it is," he said. Then he turned his back to her, drank a little more of what remained of his Scotch and settled in to observe the scene for the next fifteen or twenty minutes.

It was pretty much the same as it had been since he'd arrived. The only thing that had changed was that the dancing had grown faster. Maybe *hotter* was a better word.

Lots of bodies rubbing. Lots of moves that were almost as much fun done vertically as they'd have been if done horizontally.

The crowd was really in to it.

The wait staff, too.

He hadn't noticed them before. Now, his eye picked them up without trying. Good-looking guys, shirtless, wearing tight black trousers, laughing with the customers who were obviously joking with them, accommodating the women who flirted with them.

Good-looking women, in duplicates of Blondie's outfit—tight, low-cut, short, glittery dresses that left bare long, long legs made even longer by sky-high stilettos.

None of the women were as good-looking as Blondie.

Or maybe none of them carried themselves the same way.

She was easy to spot, even in the crowd. She had her hair piled up on top of her head in a mass of curls. Plus, there was the way she held herself. Tall. Proud. Her posture almost rigid.

Forget what she was wearing, that I'm-too-sexy-for-this-dress thing.

It was her bearing that spoke loudest, and what it said was, Keep Away.

Caleb found his eyes glued to her.

He saw what happened when she approached one of the tiny tables ringed around the dance floor and one of the bozos seated at it laughed up at her, said something, and put a hand on her hip.

She pulled back as if that hand was a scorpion.

He saw what happened when she fought her way through the mobbed dance floor with a small silver tray of drinks in her hands and another bozo cupped her bottom.

Somehow, she managed to take a step in just the right direction and sink her spiked heel into his instep.

Without spilling a drop.

Caleb smiled.

The lady could handle herself...

At least, she could until the same bozo followed her, crowded her into a small, miraculously vacant corner, and said something to her.

She shook her head.

The guy said something again. And touched her. One fast, quick grope at her breasts.

Caleb's smile faded. He stood straighter, tried to see more of what was happening but people walked by, got in the way...

Okay.

Blondie had slipped free. She was moving as fast as she could, heading for what had to be a service door.

The guy went after her.

He got to the door at the same second she did. Caught her by the shoulders. Yanked her back against him. Ground his body against hers.

She fought back.

It was useless.

The man was too big, too determined, probably too high or too drunk. Now he had one hand on her breast, the other, dammit, the other between her thighs...

Anger flashed through Caleb's blood.

Didn't anybody see what was happening? Was he the only one who understood that this wasn't a man making a fool of himself, that it was—hell, it was attempted rape?

He swung away from the balcony railing, dropped his glass on the first table he passed, went through the crowd and down the nearest staircase pretty much the same way he'd gone through linebackers in his days as a tight end on his high-school and college football teams.

Where was she?

He was tall, six foot three, but it was almost impossible to see past this mob.

The service door had been in the back of the room. On the left. He headed in that direction, not bothering with "sorry" or "excuse me" as he shoved his way across the dance floor, just doing whatever it took to get where he needed to be.

It seemed to take a lifetime but finally he broke through the crowd.

Saw the door.

But that was it.

Blondie was gone. So was the guy.

Caleb looked all around him. Nothing.

Okay.

He drew a couple of deep breaths. Some good Samaritan must have seen what was happening and put a stop to it.

Or the guy had figured he'd had his fun and given up.

Or…

Holy hell!

Somebody opened the service door, stepped back fast and let it swing shut. Elapsed time, maybe three seconds…but long enough for him to see everything he needed.

The door didn't lead to the kitchen. It led to some kind of big, dimly lit closet. A storage area, probably.

Inside, the blonde waitress was pinned against a wall, struggling against a man who towered over her.

Caleb ran to the door. Shoved it open. Said something hard and loud and absolutely ugly.

The man swung toward him.

"What the hell do you want?" he snarled. "This is none of your business. Go on, get the eff out of here!"

Caleb looked at the woman. Her eyes were enormous, her face pale despite the heavy layers of makeup. One strap of her dress was torn and the bodice was falling down.

"Are you all right?"

"He was going to—" Her voice broke. "He was going to—"

"Hey, pal. You deaf? I told you to get the eff out of—"

The man was just about Caleb's size. He had a muscled body, same as Caleb.

But there was a difference.

One of them was all lust and ego.

The other was all righteous rage.

Caleb went straight at him.

It didn't take very long. A couple of quick rights, a left to the gut and the son of a bitch staggered and clutched his belly.

"I was just having some fun," he said.

Caleb's smile was all teeth.

"So am I," he said, and hit him one last time.

That was the blow that did it. The guy fell back, hit the wall and went down it, slow and easy, until he lay right where he belonged.

On the floor, at the waitress's feet.

Caleb looked at him, wiped his hands on his trousers, then looked at the woman. She was even paler than she'd been moments ago.

"Hey," he said softly.

Her eyes flew to his.

"It's okay," he said.

He saw her throat constrict as she swallowed.

"He's—he's been after me all night."

The words were a rusty whisper. She was starting to tremble. Caleb cursed softly, stripped off his suit coat and held it toward her.

"Put this on."

"I tried to get rid of him but he wouldn't leave me alone." A shudder went through her; she looked at Caleb again. "And then he—he grabbed me. And—and he pushed me in here. And—and—"

Caleb stepped forward, started to wrap the jacket around her. She jumped at the feel of his hands.

"Easy," he said as softly as if she were one of the fillies he used to tame when he was a kid, working with the ranch hands at *El Sueño*.

Carefully, he draped his jacket around her shoulders. It covered her from her throat to her knees.

"Come on," he said. "Put your arms through the sleeves."

She did. And even more carefully, making sure he didn't let his hands brush against her, he snugged the lapels together and closed the buttons.

She trembled, but she let him do it.

Her attacker moaned.

Caleb looked down at him. The man's nose was pouring blood, and angled crookedly across his face. One eye was swollen shut.

Not enough, Caleb thought coldly.

The woman seemed to sense it. She touched his arm.

"Please, could you get me out of this place?"

"Shall I call the police?"

She shook her head.

"No. The publicity… And—and he didn't—he didn't… He never had the chance to—to do more than—than touch me. You got here before he could—" She drew a deep breath. "I just want to go home."

Caleb nodded. It was an excellent idea—until he thought of shoving through the crowd outside.

"Is there a back entrance?"

"Yes. That door, behind you… It leads to a delivery bay."

In his rage, he hadn't noticed the door but he saw it now, in the rear wall.

"I'm going to put my arm around your shoulders," he said. "Just to play it safe. Okay?"

She looked up at him. Her face was streaked with mascara. Her mouth was trembling, and he thought he had never seen a more beautiful woman in his life.

"Okay?" he repeated.

"Yes."

Caleb put his arm around her. She stiffened but she didn't pull free. They walked to the door; he pulled it open.

The street outside was dark and deserted. He'd stepped into enough streets like it, back in his Agency days, to feel every sense come alive.

"Stay close," he said softly.

She burrowed against him as the door clicked shut. She felt delicate, almost fragile in the curve of his arm.

He wanted to go back into the club and pound his fist into the face of the bastard who'd hurt her again.

But he couldn't.

She needed him.

And he needed wheels. He'd come here by taxi but from the looks of things, it might take a long time for one to cruise by.

They walked to the corner. Caleb took out his cell phone and hit the pre-programmed number for the private car service he used when he was in New York. He was in luck. One of their limousines had just dropped off somebody only a couple of blocks away.

He held her close while they waited. A couple of minutes was all it took before a long black car pulled to the curb. The driver sprang out and opened the rear door.

The girl turned toward Caleb.

"Thank you."

He smiled. "You're welcome."

"I don't even know your name."

He was tempted to say he'd introduced himself earlier but she obviously didn't remember the incident. Besides, he wasn't proud of it.

"Caleb," he said. "And you're…?"

"Sage."

The name suited her. Sage grew wild on *El Sueño*. It was strong and enduring. And beautiful. Like her. Why had he ever thought her only pretty? Even now, with black gunk under her eyes, she was lovely.

"Well," she said again, "thank you for…" She paused. Her face took on color. "Oh."

"What is it?"

"How much will the ride cost?" She patted a tiny sequined wristlet that he'd assumed was a bracelet. "I keep my money and my keys with me. Nobody trusts the lockers so—so, the thing is, I have money but I don't think it's enough to pay for—"

"Why would I let you pay?"

"No. I mean, I couldn't permit you to—"

"I was going to call for a car anyway," he said, lying through his teeth. "Seeing you home will just be a slight detour."

"Seeing me…?" She shook her head. "Going with me, you mean?"

Caleb nodded.

"Oh no," she said quickly. "Really, that isn't—"

"It is," he said, softly but with steely determination. "I'll take you to your door, make sure you're safely inside, and then I'll leave."

She nibbled at her lip. He could almost see what she was thinking. Was he going to turn into her worst nightmare, too?

"Scout's honor," he said, holding up his hand in the time-honored Boy Scout signal because he couldn't come up with any real way to convince her that his intentions were honorable.

Besides, giving things a light touch was better than giving in to the anger still boiling inside him.

Finally, she nodded. "Thank you again." She turned, started to step into the limo. At the last second, she swung toward him. "I should tell you… I live in Brooklyn."

From the way she said it, she could have been talking about Outer Mongolia.

"That's okay," he said as somberly as possible. "My inoculations are all up to date."

She stared at him for a couple of seconds. Then she laughed. It was a wobbly laugh, still, hearing it made him feel good.

"You're a nice man," she said softly.

Him? Nice? Caleb Wilde, ex-spy? Caleb Wilde, corporate attorney? He'd been called smart, even brilliant. Daring. Hell, ruthless…

"Thank you," he said, and meant it.

"You're welcome."

They smiled at each other. She cleared her throat.

"I don't—I don't like to think what would have happened if you hadn't—"

"Then don't," he said quickly. "Don't think about it, and we won't even talk about it. Deal?"

He held out his hand.

Sage looked at it. Then, slowly, she put her hand in his.

His fingers and palm swallowed hers.

No surprise, Sage thought as she got into the limo. Her rescuer was big. Not just tall but big in the way of men who were physically fit.

She was tall, too. And she was wearing spiked heels. Still, she had to tilt her head back to look at his face.

And what a face it was.

He was incredibly handsome, not in the pretty-boy way of far too many men in this city but in a way that was ruggedly masculine.

Not that any of that mattered.

Big. Brave. Fearless.

And he'd come to her rescue when nobody else had even tried. Loads of people had seen what had happened, that a man had half dragged, half carried her into that storage room.

She'd fought and kicked and pounded her fists against her attacker but the people watching had either decided it was just part of some kinky sex game or they hadn't wanted to get involved.

Someone had even opened the door, laughed and said "Hey, sorry to intrude!"

If this stranger hadn't come along…

"Sage?"

She blinked and looked at him.

"Your address," he said gently.

For a heartbeat, despite all the things she'd been think-ing, she hesitated.

Caleb put his hand over hers on the smooth leather seat.

"I promise," he said. "You can trust me."

And Sage, who had been on this earth long enough to know better, smiled tremulously at her knight in shining armor and decided that she could.

CHAPTER TWO

TRAFFIC built as they traveled through Manhattan but it thinned again once they crossed over the Brooklyn Bridge.

Now the limo moved swiftly through the dark streets.

Sage was silent. That little laugh Caleb had managed to win from her was long gone. She sat huddled in the corner of the wide leather seat, her face turned to the window. All he could see of her was the back of her head and the rigidity of her shoulders beneath his jacket.

And her long, very long legs.

Hell.

He had no business thinking about her legs. Not at a time like this.

She'd had a terrifying experience. Somehow, thinking of her as a woman was wrong right now.

What she needed was…what?

He felt helpless.

She hadn't wanted to call the cops and he understood that, but surely she needed…something.

Hot tea? Brandy? Someone to talk to? Someone to hold her? She'd let him do that but only for a minute.

He was a stranger. A male stranger. The last thing she'd want was to be in his arms. The trouble was that his every instinct told him to reach for her, draw her close, stroke her hair, let some of his strength leach into her.

She was too quiet. Too withdrawn. After that one little

laugh at his pathetic attempt at humor, she'd told the driver her address and she hadn't spoken a word since.

If only he could draw her out. Get her talking about something. Anything. He'd searched his brain for a way to start a conversation but "What do you think of the weather?" seemed woefully inadequate.

Besides, she wasn't in the mood for small talk.

The truth was, neither was he.

His jaw tightened. He was still angry as hell.

He'd let the piece of crap who'd attacked her get off easy. A man who'd force himself on a woman deserved to be beaten within an inch of his life.

Caleb let out a long breath.

Except, wiping up the floor with the bastard would only have upset her more. The best thing had been to get her out of there ASAP, and that was what he'd done.

He looked at her again. She'd drawn her legs up under her. And she was trembling.

He leaned forward.

"Driver? Turn off the AC, please."

Sage turned quickly toward him.

"No, please. Not on my account."

Caleb forced a quick smile.

"Heck," he said, trying to sound casual, "I'm doin' it for me. I'm freezin' my tail off. You northerners must have a thing for goose bumps."

Her eyes, wide and almost luminous in the shadowed interior of the limo, searched his face.

"Really?"

"Hey," he said, doing his good-ol'-boy imitation for the second time that night, doing whatever it took to keep her talking, "Ah'm from Tex-ass."

The gambit didn't work. She nodded, said "Oh," and went back to staring out the window.

Caleb gave it a couple of minutes. Then he tried again.

"So," he said with enough false cheer to make him wince, "we're in Brooklyn now, huh?"

It was a stupid question. It deserved a stupid answer. But she was too polite for that. Instead, she swung toward him.

"Yes."

He nodded wisely. "What part do you live in?"

"It's called East New York."

"Interesting name."

That won him the tiniest twitch of her lips.

"It's an interesting neighborhood."

"Meaning?"

"Have you ever been in Brooklyn before?"

"Does a housewarming party in Park Slope maybe seven, eight years back, count?" That won him a faint smile. He wanted to pump his fist in the air but he settled for smiling at her in return. "No, huh?"

"No," she replied. "Definitely not. Park Slope is upscale. It's full of lawyers and accountants and... What?"

"That's who I was visiting that night," Caleb said. "A lawyer buddy whose wife is a CPA."

"You're not going to tell me you're a CPA!"

"You're right, I'm not." He smiled. "I'm an attorney."

"I wouldn't have picked you as either."

"Why not?"

Why not, indeed?

Well, because lawyers and CPAs were supposed to be coolly logical, weren't they?

But this man had acted on pure instinct. He'd protected her. Saved her. She hated the very concept of violence but seeing him put her attacker down had thrilled her.

His behavior was so masculine. Tough but tender. The sexiest possible combination. True, she didn't know much about men, well, except for David, whom she adored, but it was impossible to imagine him taking care of her like Caleb.

She was pretty sure he was the guy who'd given her a hard

time on the balcony, but when it came to basics, he was the only man who'd looked past her awful costume and come to her rescue.

Now, he was trying to get her to relax. That's what these conversational forays were all about. She appreciated the effort but what she really wanted was to curl up in a tight ball and pretend she wasn't here, the way she used to when she was a little girl.

He wouldn't let her do that.

And he was probably right.

Pretending a thing wasn't happening hadn't worked when she was a kid. And it wasn't working right now.

"...still waiting," Caleb said.

Sage blinked. "Waiting?"

"Sure. To hear whether it's good or bad that you wouldn't have picked me for a lawyer."

He was smiling. Her heart gave a tiny extra beat. He had a wonderful smile. And he was incredibly good-looking.

"That right hook of yours," she said, shoving all that nonsense out of her head, "isn't the lawyerly type."

He laughed. "Thank you... I think."

Caleb saw her lips curve in a little smile. Excellent, but the silence crept back in. *Not good,* he thought, as his mind scrambled for some way to re-start the conversation.

Talking had been good for her. She still clutched his jacket to her hard enough that her knuckles were white, but at least her posture was a little more relaxed.

Say something, Wilde, he thought, and cleared his throat.

"So, if Park Slope is upscale, where you live is...?"

The limo slowed, pulled to the curb.

"We're here, sir," the driver said.

Caleb looked out the window. He stared at the street. At the buildings that lined it. Then he stared at Sage.

"*This* is where you live?"

Wrong tone to use. She stiffened, this time with indignation, but how else was a man to sound when he delivered a woman to her door and that door turned out to be in the middle of what could be called a slum only if you were feeling particularly generous?

They were in front of a four-story house. A charitable soul, or maybe a Realtor, might have said it was part of a historic-looking group of brick buildings.

Caleb wasn't feeling charitable, and he sure as hell wasn't a Realtor.

The building was one in a string of identical structures, strung together like beads jammed on a chain. He saw boarded-up windows. Rusted iron bars. Sagging steps that led to sagging stoops.

The street itself was long. Narrow. A couple of the streetlights were out.

The place looked like an ad for urban blight.

What he didn't see were people.

It was late, sure, but this was the city that boasted that it never slept.

"Thank you," Sage said.

Caleb swung toward her. The driver was at the door, opening it. She was getting ready to step out of the car.

"Wait a minute."

"This was very kind of you, Mister... Caleb."

He caught hold of her arm.

"I said, wait a minute!"

She hissed, jerked against his hand. Wrong move, dammit! He could almost see what she was thinking.

Carefully, he let go of her.

"I only meant... Are you sure this is the correct address?"

Her expression changed, went from fearful to defiant.

"Very sure. This is where I live."

Caleb thought of a polite way to tell her that her surroundings were dangerous, but surely she already knew that.

It didn't matter. She read his mind.

"Not quite Park Slope," she said with a thin smile.

To hell with being polite.

"No," he said bluntly, "it sure as hell isn't."

The faint smile vanished.

"Am I supposed to apologize because you don't approve?"

"No. Of course not. I only meant…" He stopped, took a long breath, let it out and started again. "Where's the subway?"

"Why?"

"Because I'm trying to picture you making this trip each night, that's why!"

"I—I usually walk home from the subway with a friend."

"She works with you?"

"No. But our work schedules are similar."

"Yeah, well, where would she have been tonight?"

It was an excellent question, and a complicated one, starting with the fact that "she" was a "he" named David.

Sage was definitely not in the mood to answer it.

"Look," she said, "I admit that this is—it's not exactly a great neighborhood. And, thanks to you, I didn't have to deal with the subway. So thank you again, here's your jacket, and—"

"Keep it," he said gruffly.

"At least give me your address so I can—"

"You can give it back to me after I get you to your door."

"No. That isn't nec—"

Caleb got out of the limo and walked around it.

"No arguments. I'm seeing you inside and that's that."

"Do you always get your own way?"

"I do when it matters."

He could almost see her weighing his words. Finally, she sighed. Some of the belligerence went out of her expression. Caleb held out his hand.

Sage hesitated, then took it.

His hand was warm, his grip powerful. She fought the desire to wind their fingers together.

The truth was, she'd run out of bravado.

His reminder that without him she'd have been walking home alone had done it, especially when she knew there'd been a recent string of assaults in the neighborhood on women who lived alone.

Not that she lived alone.

Not exactly.

The bottom line was that there was nothing to gain by pretending she didn't appreciate his help.

"Thank you," she said, as they climbed the steps to the stoop. "Again."

"There's nothing to thank me for. I'm glad to be able to help." When they reached the front door, he held out his hand. "Your keys."

She shrugged, as if it wasn't important. "The lock's broken."

He wanted to say something. She could see it. But he didn't. Instead, he nodded, opened the door...

And said something low and unpleasant.

She couldn't blame him.

She felt the same way each time she stepped into the dark, dirty entryway, inhaled the stink of beer and pee and marijuana, saw the banged-up doors that lined the hall and the wooden stairs that rose into the gloom.

Say something, she told herself, *say anything.*

"Well," she said brightly, "this is it."

He looked at her as if she were crazy.

"My apartment is on the fourth floor."

Still nothing from him. Or—wait. There was...something. A tiny glint in his blue eyes.

"What in hell are you doing in a place like this?"

She thought of half a dozen answers. Any one of them

would tell him things far more personal than he needed to know.

"I live here," she said with as much dignity as she could muster, and she started toward the stairs.

She didn't get very far before his hands closed on her shoulders and he swung her toward him.

"Dammit," he said gruffly, "cut the act! It's a good routine, pretending you're tough and street-smart, but I was there an hour ago when the price of that act got too high." She gasped as he lifted her to her toes. "Anything could happen to you here."

"Nothing has."

"Really? Is that what you call what went on tonight?"

"That had nothing to do with this."

"You *work* in a dangerous place. You *live* in a dangerous place."

"It's called doing what I can to keep a roof over my head."

"Don't you have anyone who can help you?"

"I'm doing just fine on my own."

"Oh, yeah. Yeah, I can see—"

One of the apartment doors swung open. Two men stepped into the hall. They were big and ugly; half of one's face was a blur of homemade tattoos.

Sage had seen them before. They made a habit of saying things to her, ugly things; one always made a clicking sound with his mouth when she walked by.

They scared the hell out of her .

"Whoops," the one with the tattoos said. "We breakin' up the party?"

The other grinned, two front teeth gleaming gold.

"Sure looks like it's gonna be fun."

"Sure does. You think maybe they want company?"

Caleb's hands dug into her shoulders. She could almost feel the tension radiating through him.

"Caleb," she murmured. "Don't."

"Kay-Leb," the tattooed one said in a falsetto, "don't!"
Oh God!

"Caleb," Sage said sharply. "Are you coming or not?"

"Yeah, man. You goin' with her or not? 'Cause if you ain't—"

Sage twisted free of Caleb's grasp, grabbed his hand and all but dragged him to the stairs.

He tried to shake loose. She wouldn't let him. She hung on with fierce determination and he knew that the only way he'd be able to loosen her grip would be to hurt her, and he'd sooner have slit his throat than do that.

"Dammit," he growled, "I'm not going to run away from those—those—"

They reached the first landing. She moved close to him and put her finger across his lips.

"There are two of them," she whispered. "And one of you."

He laughed. It was a hard, terrible sound and she knew that the pair downstairs could never be his equal in a fight.

Still, she couldn't let him run that risk for her. He'd already done enough, more than enough, to keep her safe tonight.

Sage acted on feminine instinct. "Yes, but what if you're wrong?"

"I'm not."

"What if you are?" she insisted. "What happens to me then?"

He looked at her.

And the downstairs door slammed shut.

The breath whooshed out of her. She went boneless with relief.

Caleb cursed softly, wrapped his arm around her and she slumped against him. She could feel his heart thudding; his body felt as if it had been forged out of steel.

Then, slowly, he let out a long breath.

"It's okay," he said softly.

She nodded, turned her face into the curve of his neck. It *was* okay, now that he was holding her.

What if he hadn't been here?

She gave a little mew of distress. He held her closer. They stood that way for long minutes. Then she drew back.

"I—I don't know what to say."

"You don't have to say anything."

"I mean, how many times can one person say thank you?"

He bent his head to hers, brushed the lightest of kisses on her mouth. There was nothing sexual in the gesture; she knew he'd meant it to be reassuring, and it was.

What would it be like if he kissed her differently, if he kissed her in a way that meant something more?

"Sage? Are you all right?"

"Yes," she said, a little breathlessly. "I'm fine."

"Okay," he said briskly. "Three more flights and you can get me out of your hair."

They climbed the remaining stairs; she stopped on the fourth-floor landing and pointed at the door ahead of them.

"That's me."

He held out his hand. "Your keys." He raised an eyebrow. "I'm assuming," he said dryly, "the lock on this door works."

She nodded. Gave him her keys. Their hands brushed; hers trembled.

His eyes narrowed. "What is it?"

She shook her head. What could she tell him? Not the truth, that once she stepped through that door and he left, she'd be alone—and that, despite the deal they'd made, the promise she'd given that she wouldn't think about what had happened at the club, she knew the scene would play and replay in her mind.

"You're frightened," he said bluntly.

"No," she said quickly, "I'm fine."

"To hell you are. And I don't blame you."

"Caleb. Really. I'm okay."

He didn't answer. Instead, he undid the lock, then blocked the doorway with his body.

In his old life, he'd learned never to walk into a place that could prove dangerous without being vigilant. This was the USA, not Iraq or Pakistan, but anything was possible—and after what had happened at the club, what had almost happened downstairs just now, all his adrenaline was flowing.

"Home sweet home," she said with a little laugh.

You could see all of it from where they stood but there was nothing sweet about it.

A shoebox of a living room. A bedroom. A bathroom. A minuscule kitchen. The place held old, tired-looking furniture but everything was scrupulously tidy.

"Stay here," he said.

He went through the rooms, one by one, and finally came back to her.

"It's clear."

He knew this was the time to say goodnight but he couldn't get the words out. And when she said, "I know it's late but— would you like some coffee?" he said yes, absolutely, coffee was just what he wanted.

It was obviously the answer she'd wanted, too. She let out a long breath.

"Good." She shut the door, set the locks. "To be honest—"

"You know what they say," Caleb said, smiling. "Honesty's the best policy."

She gave him a hesitant smile. "I don't—I don't think I could sleep just yet."

He put his hand under her chin and raised her face to his.

"You're safe now," he said softly.

"I know." She smiled again. "That's one of the dangers of being an actress. Having an overactive imagination, I mean."

"Is that what you are? An actress?"

"Uh-huh. That's why I work nights. At the club. It leaves me free for auditions."

"Would I have seen you in anything?" he said, and they both laughed, knowing it was the most clichéd of clichéd questions.

"Lately? Well, there's a commercial for Perrier and if you look really fast, I'm shopper number four at the checkout."

Caleb grinned. "Shopper number four, huh?"

"I tried for shopper two because she gets a line, but the director thought another actress was better for the part."

"His mistake."

She grinned back at him. He wanted to cheer.

"When I get my first Tony or my first Oscar, I'll point that out in my acceptance speech."

They both laughed again. Then their laughter faded. Time seemed to stretch; the room filled with heavy silence.

And with awareness.

Her awareness of him.

His, of her.

He could hear his pulse beating in his ears.

He took a quick step back.

So did she.

"Coffee coming up," she said brightly. "Just give me a minute to change, okay?"

He cleared his throat.

"No problem. I'll just—I'll just…" *What would I just? Nothing sane, if I'm not careful.*

She was gone five minutes, which was fine. It gave him time to get control of himself.

And to wonder what she was changing into.

Images flashed through his head. The kind he should have been ashamed of because there was nothing sexual about any of this, and she confirmed that when she reappeared wearing a sweatshirt and sweatpants, her face scrubbed clean, her hair loose.

How could she be even more lovely without any artifice?

"…jacket."

He blinked. She held out his suit jacket.

"I said, I'm afraid your jacket is creased."

"Oh. It's nothing. Just—just forget about—" He took the jacket, laying it over the back of an upholstered chair that had seen better days. Dammit, why couldn't he come up with a coherent sentence? "Uh, I'll just wash up, if that's okay."

"Oh, of course. I'll put on the coffee. Do you think the driver would want a cup? I could take it down to—"

"He has a thermos. Drivers from that company always—" He shook his head. Amazing. After all that had happened to her tonight, she could still think of someone else's needs. "But I'll tell him you thought of it," he said. "He'll be pleased."

Somehow, he made it to the closet-sized bathroom.

Caleb turned on the cold water.

He had to get his head together.

Sage was a good-looking woman. Hell, she was beautiful. Bottom line. So what?

She lived in a bad location. Worked in one, too. But he wasn't her protector. He wasn't her guardian.

And he didn't want a one-night stand with her, either.

She wasn't the kind of woman meant for casual sex.

He cupped his hands under the water and splashed it over his face.

"A cup of coffee," he told the mirror. "And then you're out of here, dude."

He opened the door. Went into the kitchen. Drank coffee. One cup. Fast, while she did the same thing, because yes, it really was time to put an end to this.

"Excellent coffee," he told her, with a quick smile.

"I grind the beans myself," she said, returning his smile.

"Well," he said finally.

He stood up. She did, too. They walked to the door.

It wasn't much of a door.

Hollow, not solid. No peep hole. A chain, but a chain on a door like this was like loading a gun with foam-rubber pellets.

It looked good, but it didn't serve any purpose.

"You forgot something," Sage said.

Caleb swung toward her. She held out his jacket.

"Thanks," he said, and took it from her. He hesitated. "Will you be okay?"

"I'll be fine," she said quickly. Too quickly.

"Look, maybe you should call a friend. Maybe you shouldn't be alone here tonight."

"Really, I'll be all right."

Caleb looked at the sofa. It was ugly as sin and built for a doll house, but it had a big throw pillow at one end and a blanket folded over the back.

"Looks comfortable."

She blushed. Why? Did she know what he was going to say? Because *he* knew, even before he got the words out.

"I'm staying," he said. "On that sofa. Until morning."

"No," she said, "really, that isn't—"

He took out his cell phone. Spoke to the limo driver. Told him he'd changed his plans.

"Tell your boss to bill me, and to add two hundred dollars for you. Yeah. Sure. You're welcome."

"No," Sage said again. "Wait—"

"Remember what I said about getting my own way when I want to?" Caleb unbuttoned his shirt cuffs, rolled them back. "Well, this is one of those times."

"But I'm fine. I'm safe. I'm—"

"I know some people," he said briskly. "I'll make some calls in the morning, see what we can do about finding you an apartment and a job."

"Caleb. Really—"

He lifted his hand, brushed a strand of golden hair back from her cheek.

"Here's something you need to learn about me," he said in a low voice. "I can be as stubborn as a mule."

His eyes swept over her face, lingered on her lips. The

desire to kiss her beat hard within him, but he wasn't going to do it. He was staying the night to protect her, not because he wanted her.

Liar.

He wanted her. Badly. But he wasn't going to take advantage. No way was he going to do that. He could kiss her, though. Just once…

Dammit!

"Go to bed," he said roughly. "Get some rest. We'll talk tomorrow."

She didn't argue.

He wondered if that meant she was having the same problem, if she was thinking similar thoughts…

Caleb gritted his teeth.

No way was he going to try and find out.

Instead, he watched her walk into the bedroom and close the door. Then he sat down on the sofa, kicked off his shoes, lay back. He didn't expect to sleep but, eventually, he dozed…

A sound woke him.

It was Sage, standing just outside her bedroom, watching him.

CHAPTER THREE

THE light from the street cast a soft illumination over her.

She wore the sweats he'd seen her in earlier. Her pale golden hair was tousled; her feet were bare.

She looked soft and sweet and so desirable he wanted to get to his feet, go to her and take her in his arms....

But he didn't.

She was watching him with a stillness that told him she was trying to decide what to do next.

He could only hope that decision involved him.

He kept as still as she, though every part of him was alert to her presence. He slowed his breathing, looked at her from under the screen of his lashes.

His pulse was racing. So were his thoughts.

Was she coming to him? Was she going to bend over him and kiss him? Go into his arms and part her lips to his?

Or was she simply prowling her own apartment for far less dramatic reasons? Maybe she just couldn't sleep.

Caleb waited for some answering sign. A couple of minutes went by before one came.

She looked away, then walked quietly into the kitchen.

He let out a long breath. It was a disappointment...and yet, it wasn't.

He hadn't stayed the night for sex. He'd stayed to protect her...and wanting to make love to her didn't have a damned thing to do with that.

It was greedy. Completely selfish. Altogether male. And she deserved better, if for no other reason than that she'd put her trust in him.

He had to honor that trust.

Honor, not to put too fine a point on it, was the primary principle by which he lived. It was the same for all the Wilde brothers.

Their old man had been too busy building a four-star career in the military to have been much of a father, but he'd managed to instill a basic code of ethics in his sons.

Honor. Truth. Duty.

If a man committed to those things, he could look at himself in the mirror without flinching.

A dim light went on in the kitchen.

Caleb heard the refrigerator door open, then close. Heard the delicate clink of glass against a countertop, then the whisper of liquid.

She was having a glass of water. Or milk. She was doing her best to keep the sounds to a minimum but his every sense was attuned to her.

What now? Stay where he was? Go to her? See what she needed?

See if she needed him?

He bit back a groan.

He knew the right answer this time. Shut his eyes. Roll over. Pretend he was asleep. That wasn't just right, it was logical....

But it was a little late to worry about logic, wasn't it? Because, hell, would a logical man have offered, no, insisted on spending the night on a sofa in the apartment of a woman he hardly knew?

He sat up. Ran his hands through his hair. Thought about closing the first couple of buttons of his shirt, and man, wasn't that crazy? Maybe he ought to put his jacket back on, too.

He rose to his feet and headed for the kitchen. He wasn't

particularly quiet about it—the last thing he wanted was to startle her—but even at six foot three, how much noise could a barefoot man make?

He paused at the doorway, saw her standing at the counter, an open container of milk close at hand.

Her back was to him.

Her hair streamed down her back.

Longing swept through him, hot and sharp. *Go back to that sofa,* he told himself. *Just turn away and she'll never even know you were here.*

Instead, he cleared his throat.

"Sage?"

She spun around. The glass fell from her hand to the worn linoleum and shattered into what looked like a thousand pieces.

So much for not startling her.

"Sage. Honey." Caleb rushed into the room. "It's okay. It's just me."

"Oh God, Caleb! I thought—I mean, I thought—"

She was shaking. Her face was as white as the milk.

Shards of glass were everywhere.

"Don't move," he said. "You'll cut yourself."

Too late. A tiny scarlet rivulet had joined the spill of milk.

He held out his arms.

"Come on. Let's get you out of there."

She hesitated. Then she leaned toward him, wound her arms around his neck, and he lifted her into his embrace.

God, the feel of her!

Soft. Warm. She smelled fresh and delicate, like a spring afternoon.

He could feel her breath on his throat, her hair against his face. He could feel her breasts, her belly, all of her, pressed against him.

He ached to draw her even closer. To stroke his hand down her spine, tilt her face up to his…

Stop it, he told himself.

This was wrong.

His thoughts. His hunger. Completely, totally wrong.

Maybe that was why he spoke so briskly as he carried her into the bathroom and sat her on the closed toilet.

"Okay," he said, switching on the light over the sink, "let's see that cut."

"It's nothing."

"You're probably right." He knelt and took her foot in his hands. "But let's make certain, okay?"

Her foot was small. High-arched. Her toenails were the palest shade of pink.

He wasn't into feet. Hell, what he was into was women. But he wanted to lift her foot to his mouth, kiss her instep....

A wave of hot longing shot through him.

Quickly, he stood up. Turned on the water in the sink, adjusted it in hopes the icy flow would warm.

"Okay," he said again, and winced. *Okay* seemed to have become his favorite word. "Soap? Check. Water? Check. All we need now is a washcloth, a towel and a bandage."

And a smile from Sage, who was looking at him with no readable expression on her lovely face.

He knew how to change that.

Bend to her. Bring his mouth to hers. Run his fingers into her silken hair...

"Caleb."

Her voice was soft. He shuddered under its gentle touch.

"Yeah," he said, forcing a big smile, "I know. My medical skills are limited, but—"

"Caleb." She was looking at him, her head tilted back. He could see a pulse beating in the hollow of her throat.

"What?" he said in a hoarse whisper.

She ran the tip of her tongue over her lips.

"My—my foot is fine. Really. Look. The bleeding stopped and the cut is so tiny it's barely visible.'

He tore his gaze from her face. She was right. The bleeding had stopped. All that remained of the cut, just as she'd said, was the tiniest possible scar.

What would she do if he put his mouth to it?

He swung away from her.

One more second and he'd be hard as a rock. Then what would become of honor and trust?

He drew a steadying breath, thought about cold rivers, cold lakes, cold streams.

"Washcloths," he said. "Where do you keep them?"

"Honestly, Caleb—"

"I can clean the cut with tissue but then you'd be that old joke, a woman blissfully unaware her sexy outfit is spoiled by a trailing plume of toilet paper."

She laughed, as he'd hoped she would. Good. Laughter. That was what he needed.

"Oh, I'm certainly wearing a sexy outfit," she said. "All right, you win. Washcloths are in that cupboard, on the middle shelf."

He nodded, got a washcloth from a neat stack of them, then checked the water running into the sink. It was still cold but better than it had been, and he dumped the cloth into the basin, swished it around, then wrung it out.

"Perfect," he said, squatting down in front of her and lifting up her foot again.

Sage smiled.

"What?" he said, glancing up and catching the smile.

"Only that you were right. You really can be stubborn."

He grinned.

"Told you."

He dabbed at the cut. Sage went back to watching him. His hands were big. They were clean, the nails neatly trimmed, but they weren't the hands of a man who earned his living at a desk. They were strong hands. Powerful. Masculine.

What would they feel like on her?

A rush of heat swept through her. Dammit, hadn't she thought about him enough tonight? Weren't images of this man, this stranger, what had kept her tossing in her bed?

Ridiculous, was what it was.

And it had to stop.

She cleared her throat.

"I, ah, I guess I made quite a mess."

He looked up again.

"My fault. I scared the life out of you."

"I didn't mean to wake you. I just—I couldn't sleep."

"Bad dreams?"

She shook her head. "No. I just couldn't—"

"I couldn't, either."

"No wonder. That sofa's—"

He looked up at her again.

"It didn't have a thing to do with the sofa."

His voice was low. Rough. She stared at him. Then, slowly, a soft pink glow suffused her cheeks.

She knew what he was telling her. *She* was what had kept him awake.

How would he react if she told him it was the same for her?

Her heart gave an unsteady bump. Their eyes met and held. Then he rose quickly to his feet.

"Almost finished." His tone had become brusque. "Let me just dry that cut and put a bandage on it."

"It doesn't need a bandage."

"It does. Are they in the medicine cabinet?"

She sighed. "Yes."

There was no point in arguing with him. By now, she knew that.

Her knight was a determined man. It was, she had to admit, an admirable quality, especially when all that determination was devoted to taking care of her.

Nobody had ever done that before.

Well, except, sometimes, for David—but that wasn't the same thing at all.

Caleb made her feel…protected. More than that. He made her feel cherished, which was a silly word to use because he was a veritable stranger.

And yet, that was how she felt with him.

She watched as he took a towel from the rack, took the box of bandages from the cabinet, opened one, then squatted in front of her again.

His touch was gentle. Everything about him was gentle. It surprised her, considering his size, considering the way he'd dealt with her attacker and the pair of animals in the entry hall a couple of hours ago.

And he was intensely focused. On her foot, on the inconsequential wound.

Was he always that way?

Would he be so tightly focused on a woman in bed?

She made a little sound in the back of her throat. He looked up.

"Am I hurting you?"

"No," she said quickly.

"You sure?"

Sage nodded, even though she was no longer sure about anything. How could she be, when one night, one man, had seemingly turned her existence upside down?

She wanted to touch him.

Stretch out her hand. Stroke his hair. It was short. Inky-black.

She wanted to touch his face, too. Trace her finger over those high cheekbones, that strong nose, that sensual mouth.

She wanted to look deep into his eyes, see if they were really blue, or were they black?

And those lashes. The color of soot. Thick. Long.

A woman would kill to claim those lashes.

A woman would kill to claim him.

Heat raced through her again, quick and dangerous. Was she crazy? This wasn't her thing. Picking up a stranger. Fantasizing about making love with him…

"Don't," he said.

His voice was low, the way it had been before. Now it was rough, too, like sandpaper.

Sage blinked. She felt her pulse beating high and fast in her throat. He was watching her, his eyes and mouth narrowed.

"Did you hear me? I said, don't look at me like that."

She knew what he meant. The tension in the tiny room had grown thick. She knew what he was doing, too. Warning her. Giving her the chance to turn back.

I don't know what you mean, was the simple answer, delivered not provocatively but with girlish innocence.

She was an actress. A good one, despite the paucity of credits in her résumé. She could deliver the line and make it believable.

The hell with that.

"Don't look at you how?" she said, nothing girlish or innocent in the words but rather, a woman's honest acceptance of what she wanted.

He made a sound that was almost a groan of despair.

"Sage," he said, "do you know what you're doing?"

"No," she whispered. "But I know what I want."

His eyes turned black as a moonless night. He reached for her, or she reached for him, and when he rose to his feet, she was in his arms.

He kissed her.

Not the sweet whisper of his mouth against hers as it had been before.

This time, his kiss was hungry.

His tongue sought entry and she gave it, willingly, eagerly, wanting his passion. And he gave it. No hesitancy. No caution. He was the man she'd come to know tonight, all male, all heat, all demand.

And she loved it.

She wrapped her arms around his neck. He lifted her off her feet, holding her to him, her breasts soft against his hard chest, her hips pressed to his, his erection powerful against her belly.

Her toes curled with the pleasure of it, and when his mouth left hers, she buried her face against his throat.

"Oh God," she said. "Oh God, Caleb…"

"Are you sure?" he said hoarsely.

"Yes. Yes. Yes—"

He took her mouth again, carried her into the bedroom, stood her next to the bed.

She reached for the hem of her sweatshirt.

He caught hold of her hands. Kissed them.

"I want to undress you," he said.

He did. Slowly. Raising her sweatshirt as she raised her arms. Pulling it over her head, then tossing it aside.

She felt the kiss of night air on her breasts, then the heat of his mouth, and she cried out in shocked wonder at the feel of it.

She grabbed his shirt. He shook his head.

"Not yet," he whispered, knowing that he had to see all of her before this went any further, that his control was slipping away like honey from a spoon.

"Not yet," he said again, and he hooked his thumbs into her sweatpants and drew them down her hips, down her long legs.

Ah, lord, she was exquisite.

High, rounded breasts. Slender waist. A woman's hips, lush and lovely. Those long, elegant legs. And at the juncture of her thighs, a mass of gold curls, waiting for his caress.

"Sage. You're so beautiful.…"

She reached for him again. His shirt was half-unbuttoned and now she undid the rest, her eyes never leaving his, their hot glitter burning him like flame.

He shrugged off the shirt. She gave a little hum of delight

and skimmed her hands over his muscled shoulders and chest, his six-pack abs.

He'd always taken care of his body, playing sports, training for the Agency, riding his horses. He'd done it because he believed in keeping strong and, yes, he'd done it for vanity, too.

Now, in some inexplicable way, he knew he'd done it for her, for a woman he'd never expected to meet, to know, to have.

Her hands were at his belt. His fly.

All at once, it was too much. He pushed her hands aside, gently, but there was nothing gentle in the way he undid his zipper, stepped out of his trousers and black shorts, and drew her back into his arms.

He groaned at the feel of her skin against his. At the scent of her. Woman. Soap. Arousal.

He kissed her. She dug her hands into hair, lifted herself to him. Cried out at the feel of his erection against her.

They tumbled onto the bed.

White sheets. White pillowslips. White duvet. The perfect setting for her golden skin, her golden hair....

Her innocence.

Innocence that had nothing to do with virginity but was, instead, a part of her, a sweetness of soul like the petals of a flower.

Caleb kissed her breasts. Suckled at her nipples. Heard her soft cries of pleasure as he kissed his way down the length of her, nuzzled her thighs apart, sought and found the ineffable sweetness that awaited him.

Her cries came faster.

Her hands dug into his hair.

He kissed. Nipped. Licked.

She screamed and came against his mouth.

He gave himself the exquisite pleasure of savoring the taste of her orgasm. Then he rose, moved up her body, took her mouth with his and let her taste their mingled passion on his tongue.

She moaned.

Raised her hips.

Arched against him.

He kissed her again. Then he knelt between her thighs...

And went still as stone.

No, he thought, no...

"What is it?" she whispered.

He wanted to laugh. Or cry. Maybe just do whichever came first.

"I don't have anything with me," he said. She shook her head. "Condoms, Sage. I don't have—"

She reached out her hand, lay her index finger lightly over his mouth.

"It's okay."

"No. It isn't. I—"

"It's fine, Caleb. I'm on the pill."

He let out a breath he hadn't known he'd been holding. She'd just spoken the sweetest words he'd ever heard.

"Good," he said softly. "Perfect. Absolutely per—"

She arched toward him.

He eased inside her.

She was hot. Wet. She was a miracle, just waiting for him to claim.

"Sage," he whispered.

She made a tiny, incoherent sound.

He watched as her eyes lost their focus. Watched her head toss from side to side.

He went deeper. Moved faster. Harder. Set a rhythm that transcended any he'd ever known.

He was a man who'd known lots of women. Who'd had lots of sex. Who knew the pleasure, the joy, the wonder of it...

But never like this. Never like—

Caleb's thoughts blurred.

She was trembling. Sobbing. She said his name, said it again, and then she gave a cry of such ecstasy that it drove him straight to the edge.

"Sage," he said.

Her muscles contracted around him.

She screamed, he threw back his head and they tumbled off the edge of the universe together.

Locked in each other's arms, they slept deeply and dreamlessly until something woke him.

A sound. A noise.

For a couple of seconds, he didn't know where he was.

Then the woman beside him sighed and it all came back. Meeting her. Bringing her here. Staying the night…

Making love with her.

He smiled. Bent over her sleeping form and pressed a soft kiss into her hair.

Light was coming in through the window. He could hear sounds from the street. That must have been what had wakened him.

He was accustomed to the silence of his Dallas penthouse condo, the Wilde ranch.

Could Sage grow accustomed to those same things?

The thought stunned him.

Why would he even think along those lines? Yes, he wanted to see her again, whenever he was in New York….

Unless he could see her in Dallas.

Crazy idea. Absolutely nuts.

What he needed was some coffee.

He rolled carefully from the bed, tugged on his trousers and padded, barefoot, into the kitchen.

The spill was as it had been the night before. No problem. He'd clean it up but first…

He'd said he'd find her a place to live. A job. Did it matter if he did it here or in Dallas?

"Hell, man," he whispered, "of course it matters…"

But it wouldn't hurt to make, what, an exploratory phone call. Check things out…

Caleb padded into the living room. His cell phone was on the coffee table, where he'd left it. He picked it up, went back into the kitchen, hit the button that dialed his brother, Travis.

Travis answered on the eighth ring.

"This better be good, man," he grumbled, "because it might be six in the morning in New York but here, in the real world, it's—"

"What do you know about the theater in Dallas?"

There was a few seconds of numbing silence.

"I said—"

"I heard you. What'd you do, hit your head? What the hell would I know about the theater? And why would you give a damn?"

"You're dating that redhead. The actress. Did she ever say anything about, you know, acting jobs?"

"I *was* dating her. She's not an actress, she's a singer. And what in hell are you talking about?"

What, indeed?

Caleb turned his back to the kitchen door. The last thing he wanted was for Sage to catch him making plans. Or not making them. This was just what he'd called it: an exploratory conversation. He had exploratory conversations all the time.…

Legal ones.

Never one that involved asking a woman he'd only just met to move to the town where he lived.

Hell.

What was he doing? Great sex and not enough sleep. A bad combination.

"Caleb?"

Travis sounded worried. Caleb snorted. Why wouldn't he?

"Yeah. I'm here. Look, forget what I—"

He heard the sound of the toilet flushing through the thin walls. Sage was awake. Dammit, he had to end this call—

"Who the crap are you?"

Caleb swung around. A man was standing in the kitchen doorway, staring at him. The guy was a couple of years younger than he was, smaller, but trim.

"Caleb?" Travis said.

"Later," Caleb said, and disconnected.

Great. Somebody had broken into Sage's apartment while he'd been playing pie-in-the-sky, and now he was going to have to take him on half-dressed—and, apparently, with only half his brain functioning.

"Take it easy," he said as calmly as he could. "Do the smart thing. Turn around, walk out the door—"

The intruder took a step forward.

"I asked you a question. Who are you? And what are you doing in my apartment?"

Caleb blinked. "What are you talking about? What do you mean, your apartment?"

"I mean exactly what I said, pal." The man's gaze swept over Caleb, taking in his naked chest and bare feet. "Where's Sage? What have you done to her?"

"You know Sage? And you live—you live—"

"I'm calling the cops."

"No. Wait a minute—"

"David?"

It was Sage. She stepped around the intruder, her eyes locked on Caleb.

"Caleb. Don't hurt him."

"You know this guy?"

"I told you, pal, I live here."

Caleb's gaze went to Sage. "Is that true?"

"Yes. It's true. But—"

"Sage," the intruder said, sliding his arm around her shoulders, "you're okay?"

"I'm fine." She paused. "Caleb. This is—"

"David," Caleb said, his voice flat and cold. "I heard you the first time."

"No! It isn't what you're thinking—"

Caleb gave an ugly laugh. "You don't know the half of what I'm thinking."

"Sage," David said, "what's going on? I go away overnight, I come back and I find a—a naked guy in our kitchen."

"Caleb," Sage said urgently, "there's a simple explanation for—"

"I'll bet there is," Caleb said through a tight smile. "You and lover boy here, you have an arrangement."

"No!"

"Yes." David gave an embarrassed laugh, let go of Sage and moved toward Caleb. "Hey, dude, I'm sorry. You just caught me by surprise. Arrangement or not, I probably should have phoned before I barged in." Smiling, he held out his hand. "We okay now?"

Caleb narrowed his eyes.

Hatred pumped through his veins. For this smiling SOB. For Sage. For himself, most of all, for having been such a fool.

"We're just fine," he growled, and for the second time in fewer than twelve hours, he put everything he had into a hard right hook.

Sage shrieked. Her boyfriend went down like a stone, eyes rolled up, feet in a mess of milk and glass. She dropped to her knees beside him.

"David! David, talk to me!" She looked up at Caleb, her eyes wide with disbelief. "You—you hit him. How could you do that?"

Caleb's lips drew back from his teeth.

"Hell," he said, "how could I not?"

He strode past her, got his shoes and shirt from the bedroom, his jacket and his sanity from the living room, and went straight out the door.

CHAPTER FOUR

TRAVIS Wilde stood just outside the double glass doors that led into the Dallas offices of Wilde and Wilde, Attorneys at Law.

Beyond those doors, a sea of antique red-oak flooring led to a handmade glass desk, the province of the silver-haired, always-dressed-in-black, stern-faced woman who sat behind it.

Edna Grantham—Miss Edna, unless you wanted your head sheared off—had been his brother's keeper-of-the-gate since the start of Caleb's firm.

She reminded Travis of his fourth-grade teacher, a woman with an icy disposition and little tolerance for the occasional foolishness of nine-year-old boys.

He was a grown man now, still occasionally foolish, though only when he chose to be, but old memories died hard, and Miss Edna could quell him with a look, especially when she thought it was in defense of her boss.

Travis knew, in his bones, he was not her favorite person.

Her icy looks and monosyllabic responses made it clear that she blamed him for being the guy who'd lure Caleb out of his office to go over to the Arts District for lunch at a new taco truck, for getting Caleb to leave early on Fridays for a beer at the bar around the corner, for luring him into playing hooky when Jacob was in town.

The truth was, Travis wasn't entirely guilty.

Yes, there were times Caleb could be a little stuffy. Hey, he was a lawyer.

But unless he was in court or in an important client meeting, Caleb was almost always agreeable to a little diversion.

He'd even been known to suggest them.

Miss Edna might not want to believe it but behind Caleb's lawyerly demeanor beat a true Wilde heart.

But not lately.

Lately, he was too busy to do anything. Anything that involved being with other people.

That was the reason Travis had come by this morning.

It was time to confront Caleb and ask him what the hell was going on.

He had changed.

Travis and Jake had both noticed it. So had Addison, Jake's wife, who was the second Wilde in Wilde and Wilde, Attorneys at Law. She was in the Dallas office three days a week, which meant she often saw Caleb more than they did, and she, too, said Caleb seemed different.

"He's very quiet," she said. "And a little short-tempered."

Last night, Travis had driven out to Jake and Addison's ranch for dinner.

Caleb had, of course, been invited.

"He said he's too busy," Jake said, when Travis asked if he was coming.

Too busy was Caleb's constant reply lately. That, and *I don't have time.*

Not for anything.

Dinner. Weekend barbecues. The monthly poker game that had, for crissake, been Caleb's own idea since the ice age.

He was too busy for all of it or any of it, and if you pushed, he'd get a leave-me-alone kind of look in his eyes that was as unpleasant as it was new.

The question was: Why?

Travis didn't have a clue. Neither did Jake. The one thing

they did know was that the change in their brother had started right after he'd flown to New York a couple of months ago.

He'd returned a different man.

Which was, of course, just plain crazy.

So, something was wrong, but what?

"One of you has to ask him," Addison had said last night.

The Wilde brothers were close. Always had been, always would be—but they'd always respected each other's privacy. And, of the three of them, Caleb was probably the one who'd chew on a problem longest before talking about it.

Travis got all that.

But he was getting worried. They all were. And that was the reason he was standing outside the door to his brother's office this morning.

He'd come prepared. He didn't want to seem too obvious, so he had something in his Italian leather briefcase, a set of documents, a letter…

A job, one that was different from Caleb's usual forays into corporate warfare. Luck had dropped it into his lap yesterday—and, dammit, the longer he stood out here thinking, the tougher this was starting to seem.

Travis straightened his tie. Cleared his throat. He was nervous, and he was a man who didn't know the meaning of the word.

Hell. Miss Edna was staring at him through the glass doors.

Okay. One last deep breath. One long exhalation. *Here we go,* he thought, and he pulled the doors open and marched across the sea of polished oak, took the million-mile walk to the reception desk.

"Good morning," he said briskly.

Miss Edna glanced to one side, then to the other. She half-rose from her chair and leaned forward until her face was inches from his.

"Oh, Mr. Travis," she whispered, "I am very glad to see you!"

"It's Travis. Just Travis," he said automatically. He'd been telling her that for years, to no avail. "You are?"

She nodded. "It's Mr. Caleb."

Travis's heart rate soared. "What happened?"

"Well, that is the problem, Mr. Travis. I don't know. I only know that he is not himself. It's got worse and worse and today—"

"Today?"

"Mr. Caleb had an appointment with Judge Henry. He spent weeks trying to get that appointment. And when I reminded him of it, he told me to phone the judge's clerk and cancel. Cancel, can you imagine?"

Travis could not. Caleb might goof around outside work but never, ever when it came to his practice.

"Okay," he said, even more briskly. "Please tell him I'm here."

Miss Edna blushed. A definite first.

"Perhaps it's better if you just walk in, unannounced."

"You mean, if you tell him, he's liable to say—"

"He'll say he's busy."

"Or he doesn't have the time." Travis nodded. "You're right. Okay. I'm just going to walk in on him. I'll tell him you were away from your desk."

"Tell him what you like, Mr. Travis. Do whatever it takes, but do it."

Travis nodded again. "Worry not," he said, trying for a light touch, but it didn't work. That Miss Edna was worried enough to confide in him was the clincher.

Something bad was going down.

Caleb's office was at the end of a long hall.

Travis hurried past a big conference room, a small conference room, a library, clerks' offices, a fax and printing room and an office Travis knew belonged to his sister-in-law, who wasn't in today.

He was glad she wasn't.

If things got loud, if Caleb and he reached the shouting stage, better for her not to witness it.

Caleb's door was shut. Travis counted to five, then knocked and turned the knob without waiting for a reply.

The door opened onto a room that was pure Caleb. Contemporary glass walls. Traditional Oriental carpet. Contemporary leather sofa, chairs and coffee table. Traditional—and enormous—antique wood desk.

Caleb stood at the longest wall of glass, his back to the door.

"I'm busy, Edna," he said. "Whatever it is—"

"Well, that clears up one thing," Travis said. "*You* don't have to call her 'Miss.'"

Caleb swung around.

"What are you doing here?"

"It's nice to see you, too."

Caleb nodded, forced a smile about as real as the one Travis was flashing.

"Yeah," he said, "well, it's good to see you, Trav, but—"

"But you're busy."

"Exactly."

Travis shot a pointed look at the empty surface of his brother's desk.

"Yeah. I can see that."

"What's that supposed to mean?" Caleb said, his phony smile fading.

"You're always busy lately."

Caleb folded his arms.

"Some of us are. And did you ever hear of knocking?"

"I did knock."

"What about waiting to be acknowledged? Did you ever hear of that?"

"Acknowledged," Travis said solemnly, as he walked slowly toward Caleb. "Fancy word for decidin' whether or not you're gonna see your own flesh an' blood, don't you think?"

"I'm not in the mood for the down-home routine, okay?"

"You're not in the mood for much lately."

"Okay. Enough. I don't know how you got past Edna but you did. And I've already told you, I'm—"

"Busy. Right." Travis sank into one of the chairs facing the desk. "Mind if I sit down?"

Caleb's eyes narrowed. "Listen, man, this isn't the time for fun and games."

"Because?"

"Because—because I have a meeting with a judge in—"

"Bull."

"Dammit, Travis…"

"Got a new client for you, bro."

"I have more than enough clients already."

"Corporate stuff," Travis said lazily. "This is different."

Caleb gave a thin smile.

"Shall I let you in on a secret?" His smile faded. "That's what I do. Corporate law, in case you never noticed."

Travis lifted his briefcase into his lap, opened it, took out a manila envelope and held it out. Caleb ignored it and Travis shrugged, aimed, and sailed it onto the desk.

"Take a look."

"I'm not interested."

"It's from one of my clients. A Yankee, but I try not to hold that against him. Smart. Tough. More money than God, and a pedigree that goes back to the *Mayflower*."

"Good for him. Now, if you don't mind—"

"But he has a problem. Only one heir. A son. Never did anything to make Daddy proud and now he's compounded things by dying."

"A sad tale," Caleb said coldly.

"It is, but it turns out that he did leave something for posterity. A baby, nice and snug in the belly of his pregnant mistress."

"Trav, I'm sure this is fascinating to soap-opera fans everywhere, but—"

"No more soaps, Caleb, hadn't you heard?"

Caleb took a deep breath. Something was going on here, something more than Travis's tale about a client's problems.

"Okay. Get to the point."

"I am. See, the mistress won't do what my client wants."

"Not that. I meant—"

"He wants the child. Wants it to carry his family name. Wants to raise it. Better still, adopt it."

"Adopt it?" Caleb said, caught up despite himself. Corporate law was his first love but there were times it seemed clinical. This, the situation Travis was describing, was as far from clinical as you could get.

"Exactly. He wants the lady to sign the kid over to him at birth."

Caleb snorted. "Like a car."

Travis grinned. "Exactly like a car. But she refuses. So my man wants to take her to court."

"On what grounds?"

"He says she won't be a fit mother. She has no money. No job. Lives in what he calls a hovel. Has loose morals."

"And your guy has everything. Money. Status. Power. The morality of all those stiff-necked old Pilgrims."

"Exactly." Travis paused. "The thing is, the lady does have one thing he hasn't. Well, beside the baby in her womb, of course."

"And that is?"

"She says the father wasn't my client's son."

Caleb nodded. "Interesting. "Well, DNA testing will prove—"

"She won't be tested. She won't have anything to do with

my client, won't even take his calls anymore." Travis smiled. "Which is why he needs a tough, smart attorney."

"He needs a superhero."

"Heck, man, how about a little modesty?"

"A superhero," Caleb said, ignoring the joke, "not me. And, by the way, what's he doing, looking for a Texan if he's from the east coast?"

"Well, he's not going by location, he's going by instinct. I mean, he trusts me. And he knows of you." Travis grinned. "Turns out you have quite a hot rep as a legal eagle. When he realized you and I were related—"

"Sorry, Trav. I'm not interested."

"Too busy?" Travis said. "Haven't got the time?"

Caleb glared at his brother.

"Thanks for stopping by. Next time, call first."

"And that's it?"

"That's it. I'm not interested. I already said that."

Travis rose to his feet. Walked to the door.

"You're not interested in much lately."

"Okay. I've had it. I don't know what your problem is but—"

"Yeah. I think you do."

Caleb stared at his brother. Travis had stopped smiling, and his tone had taken on a hard note. Caleb could sense the tension in him...and Travis was right.

He knew exactly what the problem was.

For weeks, ten weeks, to be exact, ever since he'd returned from New York, he'd kept both his brothers at a distance.

He'd told himself they wouldn't notice.

Such a stupid lie.

Of course, they'd noticed. And now they wanted answers.

Too bad, he thought grimly, because they weren't going to get them. How could they, when he didn't have the answers for himself?

All he had was anger and disgust.

At Sage.

Hell. *Be honest, Wilde,* he told himself.

At himself.

He heard the door shut. Breathed a sigh of relief. Travis was gone. That was something, at least, though now it left him just where he'd been before, his head full of what he could not forget.

He'd gone to bed with a woman he'd just met. God knew, he'd done that before.

He'd spent the night in her bed. He'd done that before, too.

His jaw tightened.

Except, this time the bed wasn't only the woman's. It was the bed she shared with her lover.

It made him shudder, thinking of it even now. How another man had lain between those sheets, taken the woman as he'd taken her, heard her cries, felt her heat all around him....

"Goddammit," Caleb muttered.

He looked out the wall of glass, hands jammed into his trouser pockets.

She had made a fool of him, letting him think of her as sweet, fresh and innocent when the ugly truth was that she had a lover, and they had an arrangement.

The guy slept around, and so did she.

Caleb shuddered.

Maybe he had it wrong. Maybe he was the one who'd made a fool of himself.

The deal she had with her lover was none of his business.

It was nasty, yes. Enough to make him angry, but enough to have made him lose his self-control? To have slugged the guy?

The SOB at the club had deserved a beating.

Sage's lover had simply walked into the right place at the wrong time.

And his reaction, the violence of it, was all because he'd been taken in by Sage's convincing act, by the humiliation of knowing he'd thought of taking her into his life.

That idea hadn't lasted long. How could it, when it had been so damned stupid?

But that he'd considered it at all, that he'd been such an ass...

That he still was, because he remembered what he'd felt, what he'd thought he felt, making love to her...

"Something happened in New York."

Caleb swung around. Travis was standing beside the closed door, arms folded.

"I thought you left."

"I shut the door but I'm still here."

"Well, open it again. And go."

"I'm not going anywhere. Not until you talk to me, not until you tell me what happened back east."

"I met with a client. I had a meal with an old friend. I went to a party I was too old for. Okay? You happy now?"

Travis came slowly toward him.

"I'm not a fool, Caleb. Something happened." Travis paused. "That morning when you were in New York. You called me."

"Did I?" Caleb said, as if the moment weren't forever burned into his memory.

"It was early. Six-something, your time, and—"

Caleb gave what he hoped was a casual shrug. "I don't remember."

"You called," Travis said flatly. "And you sounded... strange."

"Maybe because it didn't happen."

"Oh, it happened."

"Look, this just isn't a good day for—"

"There haven't been any. Good days, that is. Not with you. Not in a while."

"Are you done?"

"Why'd you call me? You sounded, I don't know, happy. Then, all of a sudden, you sounded—not so happy."

"Good thing you went into finance," Caleb said coldly, "because you do a lot better with numbers than words."

"No more games, man. Something happened and we want to know what it was."

"Is that a royal we or are you a committee of one?"

"That's what I am. A committee of one. I'm here for me. Jacob. Addison. That scary-as-hell dragon who guards your kingdom."

"You have too much time on your hands." Caleb went to his desk, straightened a stack of papers that didn't need straightening, eyed the manila envelope and shoved it toward his brother. "You all do, this client included. Your imaginations are working themselves into the ground."

"Did you go to see a doctor?"

Caleb looked up.

"What?"

"Some kind of specialist? Was that the reason you went east?"

Oh, hell. Caleb rubbed his forehead. "Travis. Listen—"

"Goddammit, how come that just hit me? The phone call. The way you've acted ever since..." Travis let out a long, suddenly shaky breath. "Are you sick? Sweet Jesus, if you're—if you're battling a disease and you haven't told us..."

"Ah, man." Caleb sank down in the chair behind his desk. "No," he said in a low voice. "It's nothing like that. And I'm sorry if..." He looked up, saw the worry in Travis's eyes and hated himself for having put it there. "I'm fine, Trav. I swear it. I'm just—I'm just..."

"Just what?"

Caleb stared at his brother. Then he sighed. Maybe if he talked about it, he'd get the whole ugly mess out of his system.

"Sit down," he said gruffly. "And I'll tell you."

And he did.

It didn't take very long. How could it, when the facts were so simple?

He omitted nothing.

He said he had gone to a woman's rescue and offered to see her home. It turned out she lived in a bad neighborhood—there'd been an incident in the entryway of her building that could have turned nasty and after that, he'd been reluctant to leave her alone, particularly after what she'd gone through earlier.

Travis kept nodding his head. Well, why wouldn't he? It was all logical…

"I bunked on the couch in the living room," Caleb said.

So much for logic.

"And?"

"And, she woke up and I did, too, and—and—"

"You ended up sleeping with her."

"Yes. Exactly."

Travis shrugged, a one-guy-to-another kind of shrug.

"Yeah, well, these things happen."

"Right. It happened. And then, the next morning…" Caleb cleared his throat. "The next morning, a guy walked in, looked kind of surprised to see me there. And then—and then he figured out I'd slept with what turned out to be his woman, and he apologized for walking in on us."

"Crap," Travis said, through his teeth.

"I decked him."

"Of course you did."

"I don't even know why I decked him." Caleb rose to his feet and began pacing. "I mean, it was his place. His woman. I was the intruder, not him." He ran a hand through his hair, looked at Travis. "Man, I just lost it, you know?"

"Who wouldn't?"

"It was just—it was so—so—"

"Ugly. They have an open relationship, whatever you want to call it, and that's not you."

"No. Hell, no. I mean, if I'd known I was in another man's bed, with another man's woman—"

"You thought she was all about you," Travis said gently, "but it was all about variety."

Caleb winced. "Exactly." He rubbed his hands over his face. "I don't understand why I let it bother me so damned much."

Travis stood up, clapped his brother on the shoulder.

"Don't let it. Not anymore. It was just a one-night stand. A little fun, a good time… It wasn't going to be more than that anyway. Right?"

"Right," Caleb said briskly, blocking out the rest of it, the uncomfortable realization that he'd been out of control that night, first taking Sage to bed, then punching out her lover…

…Feeling as if he'd been standing on the threshold of something new when he'd awakened with her in his arms that morning.

"Hey," Travis said. "I mean it. This was just something that happened. Put it behind you."

It was good advice, and Caleb nodded. "Everything you said makes sense."

Travis nodded, too. Looked solemn. "Travis Wilde, SPE, to the rescue."

"SPE?"

"Shrink Par Excellence. And here you thought I was only a genius when it comes to money."

Travis grinned. Caleb grinned back.

"Thank you, Dr. Wilde, " he said.

"Oh, no. You don't get off that easy. You want to show your appreciation, at least read through that file."

"What…? Oh. Your client. The one who wants to steal a baby from his dead son's mistress."

"Now, Caleb—"

Caleb laughed. "Just joking. Okay. I'll take a look. Maybe I can think of somebody to recommend because there's no way I can take this on. If nothing else, I don't have the expertise."

The men walked to the door. Smiled, shook hands, and then Travis left. Caleb sighed and went back to his desk.

Amazing, he thought as he sank into his chair, how much better he felt for having talked about New York.

He'd blown the entire incident out of proportion. Now, thanks to Travis, his head was on straight again.

A one-night stand. Nothing more, nothing less. And it was history.

Caleb opened the manila envelope. Dumped the contents on the desk. A couple of eight-by-ten glossies tumbled out, landed face-first. No matter. He was only interested in the contents of the thin file folder.

He flipped it open. Gave the first page a quick read. It was a listing of the parties involved in what was probably going to be a nasty court case.

Thomas Stinson Caldwell. Age sixty-two. Park Avenue address. Founder and president of a real estate empire valued at… Caleb gave a soft whistle. No wonder the man thought he owned the universe. Caldwell was a widower. He was the father of David Charles Caldwell, deceased. Aged twenty-eight at the time of his death eight weeks ago.

Okay. Page two. The woman…

The woman's name was Sage Dalton. She was twenty-four.

Caleb's pulse skittered. Sage? Sage and David? No. It was impossible.

He reached for the glossies. Turned them over.

The blood drained from his face.

One photo was of the guy he'd laid out in Sage's apartment.

The other—

The other was of Sage.

CHAPTER FIVE

THE ladies' lounge of the St. Regis on the Park was a sea of gilt and marble, its mirrored walls seemingly held in place by fat, obscene-looking cherubim.

An attendant, clad in a white-and-gold uniform, hovered discreetly in the background.

"If you need anything, miss, just ask," she'd said when Sage had entered a little while ago.

Sage had thanked her. Then she'd looked into that wall of mirrors…

And shuddered.

She looked awful. Or maybe that was too generous a word.

She was pale. Her eyes were huge and shadowed. Except for the slight rounding of her belly, which you couldn't see under the suit jacket she was wearing—except for that, she looked painfully thin.

Until a couple of days ago, she'd been the cliché of all clichés, tossing her cookies every morning.

And she was tired—from her pregnancy and from working double shifts at the Greek diner near her apartment in Brooklyn.

"You work double," the owner had told her bluntly, "or I get different girl."

So she worked double shifts.

She needed the money. She'd gone back to the club to collect her things and her pay, and to tell the owner she was quitting, but she didn't get the chance.

"I heard you made a scene last night," he'd said, almost as soon as she came through the door. "I don't tolerate *prima donnas,* Dalton. You're fired."

It would have been funny but nothing had seemed funny that day, or any day since.

She was, to put it nicely, a mess.

And she worried. A lot. The fact was, she worried all the time.

She had to find a safer place to live. That was priority *numero uno.* The second was to build up her savings. The pitiful amount she'd stashed away would never cover the expenses of the baby...

The baby.

Her baby.

When had those words gone from making her sick with fear to filled with hope?

She'd found out she was pregnant the old-fashioned way. First, no menstrual period. Then mornings spent bowed over the toilet.

Finally, she'd bought an early-pregnancy test kit.

"No," she'd said when she saw the results.

Half a dozen tests later, she knew there was no sense in denying reality.

The man she despised most in the world had left her with a parting gift.

Her own fault: A, for sleeping with him—not that they'd done much sleeping, she thought, her throat constricting at the memory, and, B, for not realizing you couldn't take a birth control pill on, say, Monday morning and then not take another until Tuesday late afternoon no matter how busy you were with auditions and work and classes...

But then, she hadn't been on the pill for sex, she'd been on it to regulate her cycle.

And she had certainly done that.

Sage gave a strangled laugh, saw the attendant's face in the mirror and changed the laugh to a cough.

"Summer cold," she said.

The woman didn't look convinced but then, she didn't look convinced someone like Sage should be in these plush surroundings in the first place.

Once she'd known she was pregnant, she'd paced back and forth, night and day, a caged tiger searching desperately for a way out.

She couldn't have this baby.

She had no money. No defined future. No plans beyond how to get through tomorrow.

That was the reasonable approach.

The unreasonable approach was that this tiny life was hers. It meant she'd never be alone again, meant she could bring up her child as she wished she'd been brought up, with love and hope instead of bitterness and despair.

Decision made.

She was going to have her baby.

Her baby. Only hers.

The child, the decision, had no connection to the stranger who'd made her pregnant.

Her knight-errant had turned out to be a vile, judgmental stranger, willing to think the worst of her, not even taking the time to let her explain.

Not that she'd owed him an explanation.

What had happened between them had been just—just a one-night adventure. Never mind that she'd never had a one-night adventure before, never mind that she'd hardly ever had sex before.

She was a grown woman.

And he—he was a sperm donor.

Except his "donation" had not come from a test tube but

from time spent in his arms, from caresses and sighs and pleasure....

Sage glared at herself in the mirror.

Pathetic to think about any of it. Stupid and pathetic, and proof, if she needed it, that the books she'd been reading were right.

Pregnant women were often at the mercy of their hormones and their emotions.

She took her lipstick from her purse. She was going to need more than lipstick. Good thing she'd brought blusher and a compact of pressed powder.

It was time to disguise the pallor, the dark circles, and to transform herself into a woman Thomas Caldwell could not intimidate.

She might be stupid about men and sex but she wasn't stupid about everything else. She knew why he'd chosen the St. Regis for their meeting.

In a city of elegant hotels, the St. Regis was in a class all its own. The place damn near smelled of arrogance and money.

If you were a one-percenter, it reminded you that life was good. If you were stuck with the rest of the world in that ninety-nine-percent slot, it humbled you. Put in your place.

No question, David's father was certain he knew where she belonged. To him, she was a scullery maid straight out of a bad nineteenth-century novel: broke, unwed, pregnant and desperate.

Well, three out of four wasn't bad.

But she wasn't desperate.

Things would be difficult but they'd be doable. Everything was doable, if you tried hard enough.

Bottom line? Caldwell didn't know her at all. He hadn't known his own son, not the real David, or he'd have admitted that he could never have fathered her baby.

Thomas Caldwell wasn't big on truth.

She had no idea how he'd found out she was pregnant, either.

She suspected he'd had private detectives doing their best to dig up dirt about her, once he saw how close she and David were. Maybe he'd kept them on, after David's death. And they'd followed her. Tapped her phone. For all she knew, they could have dug through her trash, found the discarded pregnancy tests.

It didn't matter.

She knew only that Caldwell had started phoning weeks ago, demanding she admit she carried his grandson—God, what a terrible thought!—and that she agree to sell the baby to him.

Of course, he wasn't fool enough to phrase it that way.

He talked about Providing What David Would Have Wanted For His Child. You could almost see the caps in the air.

When that hadn't worked, things got grim. How much did she want for the baby? One million? Two? Four? Five?

Sage dabbed blusher on her cheeks. The effect, bright pink against fish-belly white, made her look even worse. The attendant must have thought so, too, because she stepped up, silently offered a handful of tissues.

"Thank you," Sage said, and wiped the stuff off.

She'd given up telling Caldwell how wrong he was, that the baby was not David's. She'd stopped taking Caldwell's calls. Ignored the messages he left.

And it had paid off.

Last week, he'd couriered her a letter.

You win, Ms. Dalton, he'd written. *I'm done trying to change your mind. My attorney has drawn up a document stipulating that you absolve me of any and all present and future claims of lineage and inheritance. Sign it in his pres-*

*ence and mine, and in the presence of witnesses, and you will
not hear from me again.*

Which was why she was here today. And if Caldwell
wanted the pleasure of seeing her in a setting she might find
daunting, so be it.

He was in for a disappointment.

She would not be intimidated. She would only be relieved
to get him out of her life forever.

A swipe of lipstick? Not bad. Adjust the pins that held her
hair back from her face.

Sage turned and looked at the attendant.

"How do I look?"

The attendant hesitated. "Um, uh…"

"'Um, uh' is absolutely right." Sage dug in her handbag,
extracted a dollar bill, hesitated and took out another. "Thank
you," she said.

"You don't have to—"

So much for looking as if she belonged here, despite her
last year's, or maybe her last-last year's, on-sale gray suit, on-
sale gray pumps and definitely on-sale gray handbag.

"I want to," Sage said gently.

"Thank you, miss. And—good luck."

Good luck, indeed, Sage thought, as she walked across
the ornate lobby.

She had a funny feeling about this meeting. Thomas
Caldwell had been so persistent. And then, wham, he'd rolled
over.

She'd felt good about that until this morning, when she'd
suddenly thought, *Why?* Why had he rolled over?

Her footsteps slowed. The elevators were just ahead. So
was a house phone. She could call the suite number he'd
given her, tell him he could send her the papers, that she'd

have them witnessed and notarized and that he'd have to accept her doing it that way.…

Did she want him out of her life, or did she want him bothering her for the rest of it?

Sage gave herself a little shake and marched straight to the elevators.

She was meeting Caldwell in suite 1740.

For privacy, he'd said, when she'd balked and said she'd prefer meeting in the lobby.

"I have no intention of running the risk of having this matter made fodder for the media—or were you hoping for the chance at publicity?"

The elevator car was as elaborate as the lounge, all marble and gold leaf, attended by a little man who looked as if he'd stepped out of an operetta.

"Your floor, madam," he said politely, when the doors slid open.

Sage thanked him and stepped out onto gold-veined white marble. She could hear her heart pounding over the tap-tap-tap of her heels as she walked down the corridor.

The sooner this was over, the better.

She paused at the door to suite 1740. Raised her hand to knock. Lowered her hand. Raised it. Checked her watch.

She was six minutes early. So what? Get in, sign the papers, get out.

Okay. Time for one of the breathing exercise she'd learned in an acting class. Inhale, one—two—three. Hold, one—two—three-four. Exhale, one—two—three-four-five.

Better.

She squared her shoulders. Knocked. The door must have been ajar because it swung slowly open as soon as she touched it. It was like a scene in a bad movie, except the door didn't squeak. It wouldn't dare, not in this place.

"Hello?"

Nothing.

Sage took a step forward.

"Hello?"

Another step.

She was in a sitting room, sunlit and handsomely furnished, assuming you were a devotee of expensive funeral parlors. Ahead, to the right, a door to an adjoining room stood partly open.

"Mr. Caldwell?"

Still no answer. Butterflies were swarming in her stomach.

"Mr. Caldwell? I'm not in the mood for games so if there's someone here—"

A figure, blurred by the sunlight, stepped through the door from the adjoining room.

"Hello, Sage," a husky male voice said.

She knew that voice. It haunted her dreams.

"No," she said, while her heart tried to claw its way out of her throat.

"How nice to see you again."

"No," she repeated, the word a papery whisper.

She stumbled back as the figure moved away from the light and became a man.

Tall. Broad-shouldered. Lean.

"Caleb?" she whispered.

His smile was cold and cruel, and transformed his beautiful face into a dangerous mask.

"Smart girl," he said.

She said his name again. Then her eyes rolled up and she crumpled to the floor.

Caleb said a four-letter word and sprang forward. He caught Sage by the shoulders just before she went down.

Had she really fainted, or was it an act? She was good at acting; she'd proved it the night he'd spent in her bed.

In another man's bed.

No. This was real. She was limp, head rolling back as he lifted her in his arms.

Okay. He'd meant to surprise her. Catch her off-guard. Get her to admit she was after the best payoff she could get because, without question, that was her game....

Instead, he'd stunned her.

Now, he'd have to deal with high drama as well as what would undoubtedly be tears and sobs. Not that it would have any effect on him.

She felt fragile in his arms. Almost frighteningly thin. Her face was paper-white except for the dark circles under her eyes.

But the scent of her was the same.

Soft. Feminine. Delicate. And when her head drooped against his shoulder, the feel of her hair against his jaw and throat was as silken as he remembered.

How could memories of her, of that night, still matter? He knew what she was, knew she carried her dead lover's child, knew she was trying to milk his new client for as many millions as she could get.

And now, he knew that he was a damned fool for taking on the case, that she could still affect him...

She moaned.

The sound shot him back to reality.

Caleb elbowed the door shut, carried her to a brocade loveseat and lowered her on it.

"Sage."

No answer.

"Sage," he said again, his tone sharp as the blade of a knife.

"Dammit," he said through his teeth, and he stalked into the bedroom, into the bathroom, grabbed a hand towel, soaked it in cold water, wrung it out...

He had done all this before.

Brought her a wet cloth. Soothed her with it. Taken care of her, worried over her.

Yeah, but he sure as hell wasn't worrying over her now.

He needed her conscious and fully alert.

That she looked like hell, that there was a baby in her belly, meant nothing to him.

Besides, she was tough.

Nobody had to worry about her.

Mouth set in a hard line, Caleb went back into the sitting room and squatted next to the loveseat. He wiped her face with the towel, his movements brisk and impersonal.

"Come on," he said. "Open your eyes."

Her lashes fluttered. Lifted. Her eyes, dark and blurred, met his.

He dumped the wet towel on a monstrosity of a coffee table, rose and stood over her, arms crossed, legs spread, and waited.

It took a couple of seconds for her gaze to sharpen. Intensify.

Then she shot upright on the loveseat.

Fear glittered in her eyes.

Good, he thought grimly. That was precisely how he wanted her. Looking nowhere but at him, and terrified.

"What—what are you doing here?"

He flashed a tight smile.

"Such an impolite way to greet an old friend, Sage."

"What are you doing here?" Her voice had regained resonance, but he was pleased to see her hand shake as she shoved her hair back from her face. "You aren't Thomas Caldwell!"

Caleb unfolded his arms, parodied applause.

"A brilliant deduction. No. I'm not." He took a card from his pocket and tossed it in her lap. "Caleb Wilde. Thomas Caldwell's lawyer."

She picked up the card. Stared at it, then at him. Her eyes widened. A man could fall into those blue depths and drown, he thought, and hated himself for the momentary loss of focus.

"His—his lawyer? But how? How did you—"

"Just one of those lucky strokes of fate," he said coldly.

"You expect me to believe that?"

"Trust me, lady. I didn't believe it, either." His mouth twisted. "Maybe life has a bad sense of humor."

She didn't respond. He could almost see the wheels turning. Then she took a long, wobbly breath, expelled it the same uneven way, and got to her feet.

She swayed.

He almost drew her into his arms.

It had been an automatic response, he knew, an instinctive male reaction to a female in need, but that the thought had even crossed him mind infuriated him.

"Sit down."

"I'm leaving."

"You want to pass out again?" He grabbed her arm. "Dammit, sit down!"

She stared at him. Then she wrenched her arm free and sank onto the loveseat.

"Where's Caldwell?"

"Have I spoiled your plans? Were you looking forward to a face-off with a man grieving for his son?"

"Grieving?" She gave a shaky laugh. "For a lawyer, Mister—" she glanced at his card, still clutched in her hand, "for a lawyer, Caleb Wilde, you're not very smart."

"Your patsy isn't coming."

"My what?"

Caleb sat down in one of the chairs that flanked the loveseat.

"How much?"

"What?"

"How much do you want for the baby?"

"Are you crazy?"

"Look, let's not waste time. You told Caldwell you won't give him his grandchild but we both know that's bull. Tell

me your number and I'll tell you if you're anywhere in the
ball park."

She got to her feet. So did he.

"Goodbye, Mr. Wilde."

Caleb watched her through narrowed eyes. She was good,
but then, she was an actress.

"Let's get down to basics, Ms. Dalton. The last offer was
five million. I'm authorized to up it to six, no higher. Take
it or leave it.

She gave a sad laugh. "You're pitiful. You and your boss."

"He's my client."

"He can be your fairy godfather, for all I give a damn. I
came here to sign something that will get him the hell out
of my life. Nothing to sign? Then, we have nothing to discuss. And you'd better tell your client or your boss or whatever fancy name the man gives himself that if he bothers me
again, I'll charge him with harassment."

She stepped around him. He let her go, watched as she
headed for the door.

The lady was impressive but then, she'd been impressive
the night they'd met. It was an interesting combination, that
silk-over-steel quality. Her morals left a lot to be desired but
he had to respect her for having balls.

He waited until she was almost at the door.

"Ms. Dalton. You call my client's behavior harassment—
but he lost his only son. Now you're telling him he's going
to lose the only grandchild he'll ever have."

She turned and looked at him. "Why don't you ask him
when he really lost David, Mr. Wilde?"

Caleb suspected there'd been a distance between father
and son. The fact was, he didn't like Caldwell. There was
something unpleasant about the man, but that wasn't his affair. He was an attorney, not a shrink.

"Family quarrels," he said evenly, "are not my concern."

"Apparently, neither is justice."

He smiled thinly. "Trust me, Sage. You're not going to hurt my feelings."

Her chin rose. "How could I? You don't have any feel—"

He moved fast, grabbed her hands and held them at her sides.

"The feelings I have for you," he said in a rough voice, "are the ones any man would have for a woman who took him into her lover's bed."

Whatever color remained in her face drained away. "I despise you," she whispered.

"You didn't that night." He closed the inch between them, transferred both her hands to one of his and lifted her face with the other. "For all I know, you were already carrying his baby."

Tears rose in her eyes. "Go to hell!"

"Were you? Was his child in your womb that night?"

She called him a word he wouldn't have thought she'd know—but then, she knew a lot of things he wouldn't have imagined.

"You parted your legs for me," he growled, "and once I left, you parted them for him—"

Sage spat in his face.

Caleb stood very still. A dozen responses raced through his head, starting with slapping her…

And ending with hauling her into his arms, taking her back to the loveseat and burying himself inside her.

One thought was more contemptible than the last.

And she—she had brought him to this lowest level of hell.

He let go of her. Took a pristine white handkerchief from his pocket and wiped his face.

"I suppose," he said with terrible calm, "this is as good a time as any to ask a question."

She lifted her chin. Looked straight at him.

"No," she said evenly. "I'm not carrying your child. Believe me, if I were, I might have dealt differently with this pregnancy."

Caleb nodded. He'd known this didn't involve him but only a fool wouldn't ask—and only a fool would be hurt by the vehemence of her answer.

What would she say if he told her that it seemed he did have feelings, after all?

Still, the "no" was what mattered.

And it was what he'd expected.

He'd only made love to her one time—*had sex with her one time,* he thought, coldly correcting himself. And she'd assured him she was on the pill.

"Then I have only one last thing to tell you." Caleb paused. "My client will agree not to contact you again."

She blinked. "But you said—"

"With one proviso. He wants proof of paternity."

Sage threw up her hands. "Are you as deaf as he is? This baby isn't David's."

"Let's say it's for his own peace of mind."

"Can't you ever speak the truth, Mr. Wilde? He wants the test because he thinks I'm lying."

"Either way, take the test and you can put all this behind you."

"So this—this was all subterfuge."

"If the child isn't your dead lover's, you have nothing to fear."

Sage took a steadying breath.

"When does he want the test done?"

Caleb took a long white envelope from the inside pocket of his dark gray suit jacket and handed it to her.

"Tomorrow morning. Ten o'clock."

Her smile was bitter. "Are you always so damned sure life is going to go exactly your way?"

"Always," he said, but it was a lie. Life had not gone his way at all. If it had, he wouldn't be filled with anger and hate for a woman he had so recently wanted more than he'd ever wanted a woman in his life.

"What do I have to do?"

"It's all there. Details of the procedure, the location of the ob-gyn's office, her credentials. She's Chief of Obstetrics at Manhattan Hospital. Unless you'd prefer your own doctor…?"

Sage's "own doctor" was a pleasant nurse-practitioner she'd seen once at a Planned Parenthood clinic. She doubted if they even did paternity tests, plus that word, *procedure,* had a very clinical ring to it.

"I'll read through this material. If I find a problem with any of it, I'll let you know."

"The lab that will analyze the results has been provided with samples of David Caldwell's DNA." Caleb's lips thinned. "If there are samples from other men you wish to provide…"

Sage pinned Caleb with a look.

"You are," she said, "the most horrible man I've ever had the misfortune to meet."

At that, she opened the door to the suite and stomped out.

CHAPTER SIX

SAGE spent an hour reading the material Caleb had given her…and the rest of the night trying not to think about what was going to happen in the morning.

The procedure was called CVS. It involved either a catheter or a long, very sharp needle. Neither sounded pleasant.

The brochure referred to "minimal discomfort." More troubling, there was "a slight possibility" of damage to her or the baby.

That sent her in search of more information.

She turned on her laptop computer and Googled Chorionic Villi Sampling. The search led her to a website where she asked questions of a couple of women who'd gone through it.

Both said it sounded worse than it was.

More importantly, they, and their babies, had come through just fine.

It'll help if you have someone with you who cares about you, one woman typed, and the other quickly added a smiley face and a heart.

But there was no one who cared for her. There never had been, not really. Her mother had died a long time ago and the simple truth was, she'd done her maternal duty but "love" had never been part of the equation.

David was the only person who'd ever cared for her…

Until Caleb, and the night when he had been her defender, her protector, her lover.

Her accuser.

Sage looked at the blinking cursor on her computer screen, typed a quick *Thanks,* closed her computer and stood up. Her back ached. Another new thing, courtesy of pregnancy. She stretched, then went to the window.

It was dawn.

Not much sense in doing anything except getting ready for what lay ahead.

She showered, dried her hair and pulled it into a ponytail. She put on a white cotton bra and panties; old, faded jeans that were getting a little snug but still fit; and an ancient Wonder Woman T-shirt she'd found in a resale shop.

Comfort clothes, physically and emotionally. She had the feeling she was going to need some kind of comfort today.

Then she made a cup of herbal tea, sat down at the kitchen table and went through her options one last time.

If she refused to go through with the test, Thomas Caldwell would continue to intrude on her life as he waited for her baby's birth.

No. Not Thomas Caldwell.

He'd delegated her to Caleb Wilde.

He was the man who would haunt her every footstep, every breath until the baby arrived and a much simpler test finally sent him, and his client, packing.

Sage drank some of the hot tea.

She had lots to do in the next six months.

Find a place to live. Out of the city. She could never afford to raise her child in New York as a single mother. Besides, she wasn't really a city person.

The one good thing about her own childhood was the memory of green meadows, trees and country roads. She wanted those same things for her child.

So the first thing was to figure out where she wanted to live. Then she had to find a place to rent.

Mostly, she had to find a job.

The dream of becoming an actress could wait.

She had two years of college—night school—that would look good on a résumé. And she had employable skills.

She was a good waitress—she'd put in more time than seemed possible at everything from diners to delis to small, mostly ethnic restaurants.

She could sell things, too. Three Christmases spent behind the jewelry counter at Macy's were proof of that.

Bottom line? She was ready to begin her new life, and how could she do that with Caleb Wilde on her heels?

She couldn't.

And, dammit, she couldn't stop thinking about him, either.

Being in this miserable apartment didn't help. The memory of him was everywhere. The living room. The kitchen. The bedroom, where they'd made love...

No. Not love.

They'd had sex.

She understood that now but that night—that night—

"Idiot," she said in a harsh whisper.

Sex. Lust. That was it, plain and simple, the same thing that had got her mother in trouble, that had led to her birth twenty-four years ago...but with a huge difference.

She would love her baby. She already did.

All she had to do was get Caleb Wilde out of her life.

Sage spread her hand over her belly, felt the gentle rise that marked the new life within it. Then she pushed back her chair, dumped the remnants of her cold herbal tea in the sink, grabbed her purse and went out the door.

Caleb had made arrangements for Dr. Fein to have no other appointments the morning of the test.

Fein's office was in a handsome old townhouse just off Fifth Avenue on the Upper East Side.

At nine-thirty, Caleb stepped out of a taxi, went up the

steps to the door and rang the bell. A disembodied voice came over the intercom.

"Yes?"

"Caleb Wilde. I'm the attorney of record for the CVS test to be performed on—"

The door clicked open on a small, empty waiting room. The receptionist, seated behind a handsome desk, smiled pleasantly.

"Good morning, sir."

"Good morning. Is Ms. Dalton here yet?"

"She's not scheduled until ten."

Caleb nodded. He knew that. The question was, would she show up? Had she changed her mind about the test... especially now that she'd read the stuff he'd given her?

He'd read it last night.

And then he hadn't slept anything worth a damn until it was time to shower, shave and get dressed.

Which was pointless.

The procedure sounded like hell. Yes, but lots of medical procedures were unpleasant, and Sage had brought the need for this one down on her own head.

So, what was he doing here?

It turned out that the receptionist was wondering the same thing.

"Mr. Wilde?" Another professional, pleasant smile. "You're welcome to stay, sir, but I'm sure you know it isn't necessary. We're a certified facility and we absolutely guarantee a legal chain of custody."

"Yes. Of course. I, ah, I thought I'd see if Ms. Dalton keeps the appointment."

If she didn't, the receptionist said, they'd notify him.

"Of course," he said briskly. "And I do have another appointment..."

The doorbell rang. The receptionist pressed a button, the door swung open...

Sage stepped into the office.

Not yesterday's Sage, doing her best to look cool and competent in a suit and pumps. This was the Sage of that night three months back, the Sage who'd gone into her bathroom and worked whatever magic it took to make a woman look sweet and innocent.

Her face was makeup-free. Her hair was pulled back in a ponytail. She was dressed in old-looking jeans and an even older-looking T-shirt.

And she was shocked to see him.

Her eyebrows rose, her lips parted—and for one crazy moment, he thought she almost looked glad that he was there.

Wrong.

Her brows drew together, her lips turned down and she said, "What are you doing here?"

Caleb cleared his throat.

"I thought I'd—I'd stop by, just in case you had any—any questions…"

She shot him a look of such disdain that it made him flinch. Then she swept past him.

"Sage Dalton," she told the receptionist in a steady voice. "I have an appointment with Dr. Fein."

"Good morning, Ms. Dalton. The doctor will be with you shortly. I have some papers for you to fill out."

Sage took a clipboard stuffed with what looked like enough pages to fill an encyclopedia, and sat in a straight-backed chair beside a small table.

Time to leave, Caleb told himself. His presence was unnecessary. And unwanted.

He glanced at his watch.

He really did have an appointment. With Caldwell. The man had suggested breakfast but Caleb had reached the point at which the thought of breaking bread with him made his gut knot.

The appointment wasn't for another hour.

Why not stay around for a few minutes? Sage didn't want him here but what she wanted wasn't the issue. Legality was. There might be legal questions she couldn't answer.

He took a chair across from hers. She didn't look up. The room was silent, except for the scratch of her pencil.

At five of ten, she rose, went to the reception desk and handed over the forms.

At four of ten, a woman in a pale yellow smock emerged from a hallway behind the desk.

"Ms. Dalton?"

Sage got to her feet. So did Caleb.

"I'm Janet. Dr. Fein's nurse." She smiled pleasantly. "She's ready to meet with you and chat a bit before we get to the procedure. If you'll just come with me."

Sage nodded.

Caleb's jaw tightened. Her face was the color of milk, just as it had been after the attack that night.

She walked toward the nurse. Caleb hesitated, then fell in behind her. The nurse raised an eyebrow.

"And you are—"

"Caleb Wilde. I'm the attorney of record."

"Not *my* record," Sage said coldly.

"I represent the client who ordered this test."

"And?" the nurse said politely.

And, Caleb thought, *what in hell are you doing, Wilde?*

"And," he said, in his best courtroom voice, "I'm going to sit in with Ms. Dalton until it's time for the procedure."

The nurse looked at Sage. "Ms. Dalton?"

Sage shot him a look filled with hatred.

"He wants to make sure I don't change my mind and go out the back door."

"That's not—"

"Of course it is," she said. "Sit in, by all means, Mr. Wilde, while I do whatever it takes to get you out of my life."

* * *

The doctor's consulting room was small and efficient.

The doctor was the same.

She shook hands with both of them, motioned them into chairs across from hers.

"Are you sure you want to permit Mr. Wilde to be present during our chat, Sage?"

Sage shrugged her shoulders.

"It doesn't matter."

Her voice was low. Not quite as steady as before.

"Well, then," Fein said, picking up the papers Sage had filled out, "give me a moment to look these over."

Fein began to read. Sage sat straight in her chair, feet together, hands folded in her lap.

Caleb watched her. Little bits of her self-control were slipping. She was worrying her bottom lip with her teeth. Rubbing one thumb over the other.

Now, she was trembling.

Something twisted inside him.

"Sage?" he said softly.

She looked at him. He cleared his throat.

"Are you all right?"

Now she looked at him as if he were insane.

"Can I get you something? Water, maybe?"

Still no answer. He leaned toward her.

"Look," he said, his voice low, "there's nothing personal in this."

"How could there be? You're a lawyer."

Caleb winced. All the lawyer jokes in the world were in those three coldly delivered words.

"What I mean is, this has nothing to do with—with anything but Thomas Caldwell's rights."

"He has none."

"So you claim."

"So I know, Mr. Wilde, as you will, too, after today."

"Look, I'm simply trying to tell you that—"

"Do us both a favor. Don't tell me anything."

The doctor looked up, her gaze sweeping from Sage to Caleb and back again.

"Well," she said brightly, "everything seems to be in order. Sage? I just want to go over some of the fine points again."

"I understand the fine points." Sage's voice was husky. "Please, let's get this over with."

"This will only take a minute, I promise. First of all, I want to be sure you are aware that it will take approximately five days to get the results. Confirmation of paternity, based on today's test and the DNA samples of one David Caldwell, such DNA having been properly collected by—"

"Yes. I mean, I'm aware of that."

"Good. As for the procedure itself—there are two standard methods. I'll know precisely which method is preferable once I've examined you. Either is 99.99 percent accurate. Do you understand that, too?"

Sage opened her mouth. Nothing came out.

"Sage? Is that clear?"

She nodded. "Yes," she whispered.

"There's some discomfort. Nothing insurmountable but—"

"I know that, too."

She was trembling again. Her voice was scratchy. Caleb felt his hands fisting.

"Either has a small risk for mother and child. Are you sure you understand that as well, Ms. Dalton?"

Caleb watched Sage. She'd gone from trembling to shaking.

"The risk for the baby. It's very small, isn't it? I mean, when you've—when you've done this test before, have the babies—have the babies—"

"To hell with this," Caleb said, his voice sharp and clear.

"Mr. Wilde." The doctor looked at him. "I just want to be sure Ms. Dalton comprehends the—"

"She comprehends. So do I. And that's why there's not going to be any test."

"What?"

"You heard me, Doctor. We're not going through with this."

Two bright spots of color appeared in the white mask that was Sage's face.

"Is this some kind of—of horrid game? Did you set this up just to see how far I would go to get you out of my life?"

Caleb got to his feet. "Get up."

"Get up? Get up?" Her voice rose. "Do you think you can order me around? Jump me through hoops? You—you get the hell out of here, Caleb Wilde! I don't want you here. I don't need you here."

"Yes," Caleb said grimly, "you damned well do."

"Mr. Wilde. Ms. Dalton—"

"Did you read the papers I gave you? Did you really and truly read them?"

"Every word."

"Then you know that the risks are unacceptable."

He was right. They were. But what choice did she have between the devil and the deep blue sea?

"This isn't your decision."

Caleb nodded.

She was right.

It wasn't.

It was hers.

He had no legal standing here, except as his client's representative...

And as the man who had abandoned her to that client's coldly manipulative arrogance.

"You're right," Caleb said calmly. "Going through with the test isn't my decision. Authorizing it is." He looked at the doctor. "I am withdrawing that authorization. There will be no test."

"You can't do that," Sage said.

Probably not. But he was the only lawyer in the room. Who was going to make a legal argument against him?

Caleb offered a thin smile.

"I just did."

Sage got slowly to her feet.

"Damn you," she whispered. "First you make it impossible for me to refuse the test. Then you say you won't authorize it."

"And I won't."

Sage looked at the doctor. "Can he do that?"

"Well," the doctor said slowly, "well, I haven't run into this situation before—"

"If you proceed, Doctor, we won't accept the veracity of the results."

"But the chain of custody hasn't been broached."

"I don't know that. I didn't supervise the collection of David Caldwell's DNA."

"It was properly done, Mr. Wilde. Ace Laboratory is—"

"Here's the bottom line, my client will not pay for the test."

"I'll pay for it," Sage said quickly. "How much does it cost?"

Caleb looked at her. "Four thousand dollars," he said. "Have you got that kind of money?"

She stared at him. He could see a dozen different emotions warring in her eyes, everything from disbelief to anger to despair.

"I hope you can live with yourself," she said in a broken whisper, "because you are the most despicable human being I've ever known."

Caleb didn't answer. He thanked the doctor for her time, told her to bill him for whatever costs had been incurred.

Then he took Sage's arm, but she wrenched free of his hand. He reached for her again, clamped his fingers around her elbow and marched her out of the consultation room, out of the office, through the front door and to the sidewalk.

She dug her heels in and whirled toward him.

"Why?"

"I told you. The risks are too great."

"What do you give a damn about the risks?" Her hair was coming free of the band that held it; she tore the band away and tossed the hair back from her face. "I don't understand you. I don't understand anything about you!"

He gave a rough laugh.

"Hell," he said, "welcome to the club."

"You don't get to make decisions for me," she said. Tears still shone in her eyes but now, so did defiance. "I am responsible for myself."

"I know."

"I always have been!"

"Yeah. I figured that, too."

"Then, what do you think you're doing, interfering in my life?"

A warm gust of wind tossed a strand of her golden hair over her eyes. Without thinking, Caleb reached out, drew it back.

"Let me help you," he said softly.

"This is insane. You work for—"

"Caldwell is my client. He pays me for legal advice, and I'm going to advise him that it's preferable to have testing done after the baby's born, when all a lab will need is a simple, non-invasive DNA sample."

"He won't accept that."

"Yes," Caleb said with grim assurance. "He will. I'll see to it."

"He won't. And I can't get on with my life until—until this is behind me. I have to find a place to live. Get a job. Make plans for my baby. And how can I do any of that if I wake up every morning, knowing Caldwell is going to phone me, check on me, that he's going to be there like a shadow, all the time?"

"I'll take care of that."

Sage shook her head. The tears in her eyes dampened her lashes, then began to trail like tiny diamonds down her cheeks.

"Why?" she said. "Just answer that one question, okay? Why are you doing this?"

"Because it's the right thing to do."

"You didn't think so yesterday."

He smiled. "Maybe I'm a slow learner."

"You mean it, don't you?" she said, her voice filled with disbelief. "You're really going to convince him to leave me alone until after my baby is born."

"Yes."

"But why would you do that?"

A muscle knotted in his jaw. How could he have known what was real and what was a lie and have refused to admit it for so long?

"Because I think you've been telling the truth all along," he said quietly.

Her eyes widened. He reached out, started to cup her face, then dropped his hands to his sides. The last time he'd felt like this—head clear, heartbeat spiking—he'd been about to drop into the darkness of an endless plain in Afghanistan.

It was, he knew, the way his mind and body prepared for whatever lay ahead.

"The baby," he said, "isn't David's."

Silence. Then Sage drew a shaky breath. "No."

Caleb nodded.

"I asked you this yesterday," he said. "Now I'm asking it again." He reached out to her, cupped her shoulders. "Sage. Is the baby mine?"

He waited, knowing this was the question he should have asked from the beginning, not phrased it as a throwaway line the way he'd done yesterday but asked with concern and meaning.

"Tell me the truth," he said softly. "Is this my child?"

Her mouth, the mouth he still remembered as tasting like the sweetest honey, trembled.

She sighed, and everything a man could dream or imagine or, dammit, fear, was in that soft, perfect sound.

"Yes," she said, "it is. I'm carrying your child."

CHAPTER SEVEN

CALEB had heard people describe transitional moments in their lives in ways that struck him as overblown, even foolish.

He knew that sayings like "the world stood still," or "the earth shifted," or that all-time favorite, "time stopped," were metaphors.

Still, what logical man wouldn't smile a little at such creaky old saws?

Now, hearing Sage's sigh, seeing the darkness in her eyes, he knew that none of those phrases were overblown, and they certainly weren't foolish.

They were accurate because if the earth hadn't just shifted under his feet, Manhattan was in the midst of an earthquake.

He had asked a question he'd never imagined asking, and the answer was a life-changer.

He knew he was supposed to say something, but what? His brain was on hold, his tongue was glued to the roof of his mouth.

In a movie, he'd have said, "I love you, Sage. Marry me, and we'll live happily forever after." And she'd have thrown herself into his waiting arms and said, "Yes, oh yes, I will!"

Music up, roll credits.

Except this wasn't a film, he wasn't Tom Hanks and she wasn't Meg Ryan.

This was real life, they hardly knew each other except in

the biblical sense of the word—and that was what had gotten him into this situation in the first place.

A rush of ice water seemed to pour through his veins.

He wasn't interested in marrying anybody, not for a long, long time. And when he did, it wouldn't be to a woman who was, basically, a total stranger.

So, it wasn't a proposal that came out of his mouth. It was something far more basic.

"You said you were on the pill."

"I was." Her words were clipped. "And it's 99.9 percent effective, says the little brochure that comes with it."

"Yeah. Okay. But—"

"But it turns out I'm that one percent. Sorry. That point-one percent." She made a sound he suspected was supposed to be a laugh. "Terrific, right? A thing works virtually all the time…except when it doesn't." She looked at him, saw the expression on his face and her chin came up. "You know what? If you didn't want to know, or if you don't want to believe me, you shouldn't have asked."

She was right.

And the amazing thing, or maybe the not-so-amazing thing was, he believed her.

On a pragmatic level, why else would she have been fully prepared to take the CVS test?

And on a level that had nothing to do with pragmatism, Sage was the woman he'd held in his arms that fateful night. No matter what her "arrangement" with David Caldwell, Caleb knew she wouldn't lie, especially about something like this.

"I believe you," he said quietly. "It's just—it's a lot to take in."

Sage wanted to say something clever and pithy, but remembering her own initial reaction to seeing those little test strips turn blue took the fight right out of her.

"I know." Her voice was low. "I absolutely know."

He nodded. "So, we have to talk."

"There's nothing to talk about."

"You're pregnant," he said flatly. "I'm responsible for that pregnancy. Seems to me we have a lot to talk about."

She wasn't surprised.

Caleb Wilde wasn't only a man who'd just learned something shocking, he was a lawyer. He'd have a speech to make, probably papers for her to sign.

Out of the frying pan and into the fire. With one huge difference.

Thomas Caldwell wanted to force himself into her life.

Caleb Wilde would want to keep himself out of it.

And that was fine with her.

He suggested they go to his hotel.

She thought of the ugly suite with its pretensions of grandeur and shook her head.

"Forget that. There's a coffee shop right next to the subway station."

"Right," he said calmly. "What better place to discuss the fact that you're pregnant than a coffee shop? We can always elicit advice from the waitress."

She wanted to tell him that *she* wasn't pregnant, *they* were. But she knew that wasn't true; men talked about being pregnant in TV sit-coms, where they were always thrilled to find out they were on their way to becoming fathers.

This was real life, and she knew, firsthand, how that went.

"I don't like your hotel room."

"You haven't seen it."

"Of course I saw it. Just yesterday."

"Caldwell made those arrangements, not me. I'm staying at—"

"I don't care where you're staying. I don't want to go there."

Caleb raised an eyebrow. "What is this, a turf war?"

"Of course not," she said quickly—except…it was.

No way was she going to give him any kind of psychological advantage.

"Fine," he said grimly. "We'll go to your place."

The scene of the crime, she thought, and felt a rush of color flood her face.

"We can talk here. I mean, we don't have much to talk about. I already told you, I'm not going to ask anything of you or—"

His hands closed on her elbows and he raised her to her toes. New Yorkers, whose day-to-day survival skills made them blind to almost everything, flowed around them like water around a boulder in a stream.

"This isn't about you or me," he said, each word clipped. "It's about this—this situation we created."

"It's a baby," she said, trying to keep her voice from quavering, "not a situation."

"You know what I mean."

"What I know," she said, "is that I've already reached a decision."

"You made that decision without consulting me."

"You're not part of this."

He laughed, although the sound wasn't pleasant.

"You're carrying my kid. I intend to do the right thing about him. Her. It."

Hell, he was getting lost in syntax, and what did syntax matter at a time like this?

"The right thing." She looked at him. "What, exactly, does that mean?"

"You want an honest answer?" For the first time, he looked less than certain. "I don't know. And that's what we have to talk about."

She nodded.

And, dammit, he thought, were those tears rising in her eyes?

A fist seemed to close around his heart. She looked so young, so lost, so vulnerable.

Without thinking, he bent his head and brushed his lips lightly over hers.

A mistake. He knew it instantly, even as her mouth softened under his.

Kissing her brought back unwanted memories. Her taste. Her feel. The rightness of having her in his arms...

Caleb turned away. A taxi was heading toward them. Perfect timing. He hailed it, then looked at Sage. Her face was pale. Her mouth was trembling. He wanted to kiss her again...

"Let's go," he said briskly.

A moment later, they were en route to Brooklyn.

Her neighborhood didn't look any better than the last time.

In fact, it looked worse.

Half a dozen overflowing trash cans stood at the curb. One had fallen over and garbage lay strewn beside it.

A pack of boys, sixteen, maybe seventeen years old, were lounging in front of the building. Two of them elbowed each other as Sage stepped from the cab.

Caleb was right on her heels.

One look from him, the kids turned away.

He figured that what he was feeling—a growing anger to replace the foolish tenderness or whatever you wanted to call it that had overtaken him outside Fein's office—was showing, loud and clear, on his face.

He grasped Sage's elbow, marched her up the steps, into the misery of the entry hall, then up the dark, creaking stairs to her apartment.

"Keys," he said, ignoring the roll of her eyes as she handed them over. Once inside the living room, he wasted no time on niceties and pointed to the sofa. "Sit."

Sage folded her arms.

"Did you hear me? I said—"

"Do I look like a poodle to you?"

Dammit, as angry as he was, he wanted to laugh, but he wasn't that foolish.

Instead, he bared his teeth in a cold smile.

"Very funny."

"No," she said, "it isn't funny at all." She strode past him to the kitchen, banged open cupboards, took out a mug and a box of tea bags, filled a kettle with water. Caleb, following after her, muttered something under his breath, snatched the kettle from her hand, slapped it onto the stove.

"What the hell do you think you're doing?"

"I'm making tea. Herbal tea." She looked up into his eyes, fluttered her lashes, gave him a smile sweet enough to cause a sugar high. "Why? Did you want some?"

Was she deliberately trying to infuriate him? He wanted to grab her by the shoulders and shake some sense into her...

Or maybe haul her against him and kiss her until sense was the last thing either of them needed.

Hell.

Where did logic go when he was with her? It seemed to disappear like smoke on a breeze. He couldn't let that happen. Again. Once was enough. More than enough. Just look where it had taken him...

Taken them.

He had to remember that.

"As a matter of fact," he said, "I'd love some tea."

He forced what he hoped was a bland smile. Then he took off his suit coat, undid the top button of his shirt, tugged at his tie, unbuttoned his cuffs, rolled up his sleeves...

"Why not make yourself at home?" Sage said in that same, sugar-laden voice.

He flashed another empty smile.

"Thanks," he said, pulling a chair out from the table, "I will."

She narrowed her eyes to slits as he sat down, stretched out his legs, crossed his feet at the ankles. When he folded his arms over his chest, she muttered something.

He wanted to laugh.

What she'd said was incredibly rude, especially coming from that soft-looking, sweet-tasting mouth, but he couldn't blame her.

He agreed with the sentiment.

Talk about things being all fouled up…

The kettle screamed. Sage dumped tea bags in a pair of mugs. He hated tea—tea was for sick people—and this wasn't even tea, it was herbal goop.

His sisters would have approved—and if there was anything he didn't want to think about right now, it was his sisters. Or his brothers. Or anybody in his family.

Anger was busy tying his gut into a knot. Why not add herbal tea and all its connotations so that the knot could tighten?

"This," he said when she plunked the mugs on the table, "is not tea."

"It's what I drink."

"Ridiculous," he snorted.

She looked at him. "Honey?"

"What?"

Her smile would have shamed the Cheshire cat.

"Do you take honey in your tea?"

"How about sugar?"

"I've given up white sugar."

"No sugar. No tea. What are you, a health nut?"

She pulled out a chair, sat down across from him.

"I'm pregnant."

"So we've established."

"Are you stupid or just out of touch with reality? Pregnant women aren't supposed to have caffeine! They're supposed to watch what they eat! Natural foods! Organic foods! Honey! Herbal tea! Get it?"

He could almost see each exclamation point in the air.

"Oh."

"Oh? *Oh?* Is that all you can say about making a horse's ass of yourself?"

"Hey. I didn't—" He cleared his throat. "I didn't know. I mean, I don't know anything about—about being pregnant..."

"No," she said and just that quickly, he saw her anger drain away. She put her elbows on the table, leaned her forehead against her fists. "No," she said again, "neither do I."

Tears rolled down her cheeks. Caleb rose, tore a paper towel from a roll that hung over the sink, and gave it to her.

"Sage," he said softly, squatting down beside her, "I'm sorry."

She took the towel from him, blew her nose loudly.

"No, it's not your fault. I dropped this thing on you like a—like a brick. I know you're—you're trying to process it."

Caleb pulled his chair next to hers, sat, reached for her hands and clasped them tightly in his.

"Look, we're both new to this."

"The understatement of the year," she said with a watery laugh.

"But we'll learn." He smiled, leaned forward, let go of one of her hands so he could tuck a stray curl back from her temple. "Heck, look how much *I* just learned. No caffeine. Honey. Herbs. I mean, you're looking at a guy who thinks that all you need in a kitchen is a coffeepot, a couple of stale bagels, some cream cheese that hasn't gone green and a stack of takeout menus."

She laughed. It was a real laugh this time, and he wanted to cheer. Instead, he moved her tea mug so it was in front of her.

"Come on. Take a sip. Good. And another. Excellent. Are you hungry? Shall I make you something to eat?"

"Caleb—"

"No? Okay. Just the tea, then—"

"Caleb." She put down the mug down. "What you said. About us having to talk…"

"Yeah." He sat back. "We do."

Sage nodded. "I just want you to know—I mean, I truly don't expect—"

"Listen," he said, "we're two adults. We have to deal with this."

Another bob of her head. Okay. This was progress. They were both calmer. Much calmer. He certainly was.

All his anger…

It hadn't been about her or even about him, it had been about not knowing the next logical steps to take, and that was rough. Law school. The Agency. His successful practice. Logical choices for a logical approach to life.

She pushed back her chair. "Just give me a minute."

"No. We can't keep putting this off."

"Lesson two about pregnancy," she said with a quick smile. "It makes you pee a lot."

"Oh," he said again. That seemed to be his word of the day.

He watched her walk out of the kitchen. She was so damned proud. So determined not to need him or anybody else.

Dammit, what was he supposed to do next?

He knew the legal choices. But what about feelings? Emotions? No way to tuck them into neat legal categories.

He heard the toilet flush. Heard water run in the sink. Heard the bathroom door open.

Sage walked into the kitchen.

She'd washed her face. Combed her hair.

He felt his heart do something—well, something weird. It turned over. Or maybe it lifted. Whatever, it was a strange sensation.

It had to be his gut, not his heart. He hadn't eaten anything this morning. He hadn't even had coffee.

He reached for his mug of tea. Drank some. Tried not to gag.

Sage laughed. He looked up.

"You look as if you're eating worms."

"Hey, worms aren't so bad." He grinned at the expression on her face. "Grow up with a couple of brothers who're always ready for a dare, you end up doing a lot of things you don't generally talk about in polite company."

She sat down across from him. No laughter now.

"Like what to do when you find out the woman you—you were with is pregnant."

"The woman I made love with," Caleb said in a low voice.

Their eyes met. After a long few seconds, she looked away, caught her bottom lip between her teeth. He watched, and tried not to think about how soft and sweet her flesh was there.

"So," she said, "so…I've been making plans. Well, I've been trying to but with Caldwell hounding me—"

"Forget Caldwell." Hell, why did his voice sound so rough? "Forget him," he repeated. "He's not going to bother you again."

"Are you sure?"

"Yes. I'll take care of it."

"Thank you."

"Don't thank me," he said, his voice even rougher. "It's just the right thing to do." He cleared his throat. "What plans have you been making?"

"The first, the one at the top of the list…" She sat forward, her hands wrapped around the mug of tea, her eyes bright. "I'm moving out of here."

"Damned right you are."

"I'm going to look for a place in—well, I'm still not sure. I thought maybe Queens. Or Long Island. Maybe even New—"

"A house," Caleb said. "A kid needs a yard. A dog. Space to run in."

"I thought about a house but renting is probably—"

"Renting isn't a good idea. It might be now, considering the economy, but by the same token, there are houses on the market that are excellent values."

Sweet Jesus.

Travis would be proud of him. Or maybe not. He sounded more like a stuffed three-piece suit than a man who was about to become a—about to become a—

"Maybe," Sage said, "but I have to be realistic."

"Absolutely. Being realistic is my specialty." *Had he actually said that?* "What I mean is, I'll draw up some plans and—What?"

Sage's eyes had narrowed. She was good at narrowing them; he'd noticed that about her, and it inevitably presaged an oncoming storm.

"I've been drawing up plans for almost three months."

"I'm sure you have, but—"

"There is no *but,* Caleb. I'm the one who's been dealing with this—what did you call it? This 'situation.'"

"While I was oblivious to it." He could feel a little curl of anger forming again. "Which brings me to a question. Why didn't you contact me when you realized you were pregnant?"

"For starters, I didn't know your last name. I didn't know anything about you, except that you lived in Texas. What we did…what I did…" Color striped her cheeks. "I still can't believe it. And believe me, I'm not proud of that."

Images flashed through his head. Waking in the middle of the night, his body on fire for her. Trying to ignore what he felt and then the realization that she wanted him as much as he wanted her, and then her in his arms, hot and wild in his arms…

"I don't regret that night," he said, his voice husky. "Neither should you."

She stared at him. Then she shot to her feet.

"I don't want to talk about it."

Caleb rose, too. He stood beside her, too close, too masculine, too everything she had tried so hard to forget.

"That's why we're here," he said. "To talk about it."

"About—about the baby. Not about—"

"I never stopped thinking about you," he said. "I couldn't get you out of my mind."

"Stop!" Sage closed her eyes, as if that might make this all go away. "I don't want to—to—"

"Hell, no! Neither do I." He put his hand in her hair, turned her face up to his; hair fell in a silk swirl over his fingers. "But I can't stop it. Memories of you. How you tasted. How you felt. How it was, to be inside you…"

She slapped at his hand.

He clasped her face. Raised it to his.

"No," she said sharply, but it was too late.

His mouth was on hers and he was kissing her, kissing her with weeks of pent-up desire, with passion and yet with tenderness.

His tongue sought entry into the sweetness of her mouth and she moaned, parted her lips and let him in.

An eternity later, he raised his head, but he didn't let go of her.

"Why didn't you tell me yesterday?" He knew there was an edge to his voice. So what? What he'd just done wasn't logical but surely this question was. "You were going to go through with a paternity test rather than tell me the truth?"

"Let go of me."

"Answer the question. Why didn't you tell me yesterday?"

"You weren't much interested in the truth three months ago. Why would you have wanted to hear it yesterday?"

"What's that supposed to mean?"

"You walked out of here that night. No questions, nothing. You just—you just slugged David, told me what you thought of me, and you were gone."

"And?"

"What do you mean, *and?* That was how things ended between us. Now you're saying that when I found you waiting for me in that hotel yesterday I should have stuck out my hand, smiled and said, 'Hello, Mr. Wilde, it's nice to see you again and oh, by the way, I'm carrying your child?'" She jerked free of his hands, eyes flashing with defiance and anger... or was it pain? "What a fantastic conversation-starter that would have been!"

He wanted to tell her she was wrong—but she wasn't. He would never have believed her. He wasn't even sure why he believed her now.

Except, he did.

The events of the morning had changed everything.

She was, once again, the woman he'd met that night almost three months ago, a heart-aching combination of vulnerability and courage, and she touched something in him no woman ever had.

"I shouldn't have stormed out of here that night," he said quietly. "God knows, I was in no position to make moral judgments."

"Nobody's in a position to make moral judgments," she said tightly, "especially without asking a couple of questions first."

A muscle in his jaw flickered. "What was there to ask?"

"Never mind," she said wearily. "It doesn't matter."

"The hell it doesn't."

She looked up at him, weighing his words. Then she flashed a bitter smile. "Okay. How about, Were David and I lovers?"

"Are you saying you weren't?"

"Would you believe me if I did?"

Something stirred inside him. "Try me." Time slipped by. Caleb cursed, clasped her shoulders again. "Dammit, Sage, I want the truth. Were you lovers?"

"No." Tears rose in her eyes. "He was my friend. My best fr—"

Her voice broke. Caleb wanted to draw her against him and offer comfort but he couldn't.

Not yet. Not until the images of her with Caldwell were blanked from his mind.

"It was the worst day of my life," she whispered. "Losing him."

He nodded. Searched for words of solace…and instead heard himself say, "Why were you living together?"

She gave a snort of disbelief.

"Is that all you and your oversized ego can worry about?"

"Answer the question," he said coldly, knowing that the ghost living inside him, the Agency operative who'd been trained to trust no one, to reject answers when they weren't the answers he expected, had suddenly taken over.

"We weren't living together. Not the way you mean. David needed a place to stay. I said he could stay with me until he found something."

"So, you're saying you were roommates?"

There it was again, that quick narrowing of her eyes.

"I'm not *saying* it, I'm *stating* it. We were friends. Period. Full stop. End of story."

Caleb nodded again. One more question. He hated himself for needing to ask it—but he had to know. Dear God, he had to know if he needed to be jealous of a dead man, and if that wasn't pathetic, what was?

"And where did he sleep?"

The breath hissed from between her teeth.

"Damn you, Caleb! I don't know why I bothered with this. You're not interested in the truth!"

"Where?" he demanded, because, sure, he had female friends, he knew men and women could like each other without sex ever entering the equation, but how could a man be near this woman and not want her, not need to touch her?

"He slept where you did," she said, her voice tight. "We joked that it was the guest bedroom."

"'We,'" he heard himself say.

She turned her face up to his. Were her eyes bright with tears or with anger?

"We," she said. "Absolutely. Because David was more than my friend. He was—he was my family, the brother I never had. He was always there for me, always, until he stepped off a bus one dark night and a car ran a light and—and—"

"Dammit," Caleb said in a rough voice. He reached for her, but she pulled away.

"David and I didn't have a sexual thing going between us. We never did, never would, never could. He was gay!"

Gay. The word seemed to echo through the sudden quiet.

"Gay?" Caleb said.

"Gay," Sage said. She swiped at her tears and gave him a look he knew he'd never forget. "And you—you are a one-hundred-percent gold-plated jerk!"

She whirled away and marched into the bedroom. The door slammed shut.

Caleb didn't move.

He couldn't have, not even if a fire truck had materialized in the center of the kitchen.

David Caldwell was gay. He'd never been Sage's lover.

And he, Caleb Wilde, was… Yeah. Okay. He was a gold-plated jerk.

But he was more than that.

He was—he was—

That was the instant it really hit.

Forget polite phrases about how he had willingly admitted he'd made Sage pregnant, how he was responsible for the life in her womb. All those lofty bits of philosophy were true, but they skirted the real issue.

Caleb sank into his chair.

He was—*holy hell!*

He was going to be a father.

CHAPTER EIGHT

Sage slammed the bathroom door.

She was breathing hard. She was breathing fire!

She wasn't sure which of them was the worst fool, she or Caleb.

It had never occurred to him to ask the slightest question about that night. About whether maybe, just maybe he'd read things wrong.

But then, why would he? She'd met him at, what, nine o'clock? Brought him home with her at ten. Slept with him at whatever unholy hour she'd gone sashaying into the living room, figuring he was asleep…

Or maybe hoping he wasn't asleep.

Not that it mattered.

She'd had sex with him. Sex, plain and simple. It hadn't meant a thing to him and it certainly hadn't meant a thing to her.…

Liar. Liar. Liar! It had meant everything. At least, she'd believed it had.

Now, she carried his baby.

God, what a mess!

Twenty-four hours ago, when she'd walked into the hotel room and found him waiting, she'd figured things couldn't get much worse.

What a joke. And it was her fault.

Why had she told him the truth? Yesterday, when he'd

asked if he'd made her pregnant, she hadn't so much as hesitated. The lie had come as easily as breath.

No, she'd said, *you didn't.*

So, what had changed?

Not a damn thing, except for her sudden inability to keep her mouth shut. Telling him the truth only complicated things. Nothing good would come of it, she of all people knew that.

She was repeating her mother's story, meeting some guy, having sex, getting pregnant—"knocked up," to use her mother's blunt terminology.

Sage stared at herself in the mirror.

That she, of all people, should bring a baby into this world bearing the stigma of illegitimacy…

She knew that was an increasingly old-fashioned attitude. Not for her. Illegitimacy had defined her childhood, growing up in a small, very conservative town with a mother incapable of leaving the past behind.

Was that was why she'd admitted the truth to Caleb? Had part of her hoped he'd hear the news and say…

What?

That he'd acknowledge the baby as his own? Assume a father's role? A part-time role, at best. Alternate weekends, two weeks in the summer? Father-daughter dances, or father-son camping trips? Show up once in a while so that when other kids said, "This is my dad," her child wouldn't have to stand silent?

Sage sank down on the closed toilet seat.

All these weeks, she'd kept from thinking about things like that. She'd concentrated on the day-to-day stuff. Finding a place to live. Finding a job.

Had it been deliberate? Had she been trying to avoid remembering her own childhood? No father. Not even a name or a picture, only her mother's never-ending references to how her life had been ruined by a man.

"He was a liar," she'd say, "just like all men, sayin' and

doin' whatever would get him into my pants. Any woman puts her trust in a man is a fool and deserves whatever she gets."

It was a blunt, harsh recitation of the facts of life, but it was effective.

Sage had seen its validity all around her, starting in high school with girls who lost their hearts to boys who lied to get what they wanted and going all the way up to young actresses who fell for the I'm-going-to-make-you-a-star lies of producers.

As for sex…

She'd tried it. Once. Her first year in New York, mostly because she was tired of hearing girls say how great it was, but it wasn't great at all so she'd never tried it again…

Until that night three months ago, when it turned out that sex was—it was wonderful, with the right man, except he'd turned out to be exactly the kind her mother had described, out for sex and nothing else.

"Sage?"

The knock at the door jolted her.

She leaped to her feet, turned on the water, made it sound as if she were doing something useful instead of trying to stop her world from spinning completely out of control.

"Sage? Are you okay?"

She almost laughed. She was fine, aside from being pregnant, alone and baffled as to why she'd told Caleb a truth he surely hadn't wanted to know.

"Yes," she said brightly. "Just give me a minute."

She clutched the edge of the sink, bowed her head, took a couple of breaths.

There was some old saying about the truth setting you free, but that was the thing with old sayings.

Sometimes, they just didn't make sense.

Back to square one. Why had she told him?

Maybe it was the way he'd taken charge of things today. It wasn't just that he'd supported her sudden decision not to take the test, it was that he'd flat-out said he refused to let her take it.

It had been a kind of pronouncement.

I am Caleb Wilde. And I am in command here.

The twenty-first-century woman in her should have balked, but she'd loved that he'd made her feel safe and wanted. He'd been her knight again, if only for a little while.

"Sage!" The doorknob rattled. "If you're sick—"

She stood straight, looked her reflection in the eye, then turned to the door, unlocked it and flung it open.

"I'm fine," she said calmly.

He didn't look convinced. Well, why would he? She'd seen herself in the mirror. Her face was pale, her hair was lank; she looked like the "before" part of a vitamin ad.

"In that case," he said, "we need to talk."

"We *did* talk."

"Not yet."

Here it was. The handsome, rich, sometimes-nice, some-times-not-nice guy she'd let turn her world inside-out was about to throw money at her in return for her promise to dis-appear from his life.

It was an approach better than that of her own biological father, but not by much.

"Look," she said wearily, "let's just cut to the chase, okay? I know what you're going to say."

"Wow. Such a useful talent."

"And I can save you a lot of time. I want—"

"You told me. A place to live. A job. Now, it's my turn."

What she wanted was for him to go away but, okay, let him talk. She knew she'd never get rid of him until she did.

"Fine," she said, and swept past him into the cramped liv-ing room.

Swept, Caleb decided, was the only word for it.

How a woman in jeans and a T-shirt could seem regal was

beyond him to comprehend, but then, pretty much everything about this particular woman was in that category.

He'd never met a woman like her, and whether that was good or bad was still up for grabs.

She took a chair.

He took the couch.

She sat straight, knees together, hands locked in her lap. She was pale, but other than that, she seemed okay.

She'd been in the bathroom for so long, he'd started to wonder if she was sick. Didn't pregnant women get sick easily? The queasy-belly thing?

He didn't know a thing about pregnant women.

His three sisters were busy with their careers. Jake was a newlywed. Travis was—well, he was Travis. It would be a miracle if he ever settled on one woman, let alone decided to become a father.

Not that he, Caleb, had made any such decision. This thing had been an accident, but if he'd been looking for a woman, for one to have a child with, Sage would have been a good choice.

Maybe a perfect choice.

She was bright. Interesting. Brave. And she was fun. Well, fun when she wasn't going toe-to-toe with him and arguing, but the truth was, he liked that about her.

Women never argued with him.

They pretty much agreed with whatever he said. His sisters teased him about it.

Must be nice to be king, Em had said, giggling, after she'd overheard one of his dates breathlessly assuring him that he was absolutely right about some political thing she'd probably never heard of until he'd mentioned it.

Added to all that, Sage was, well, she was beautiful.

Hair like sunlight. Eyes like the sea. Clichéd, but true. A rose-pink mouth that could curve into a smile or tremble with emotion, and that tasted indescribably sweet.

She was damn near shapeless within that T-shirt but he didn't have to see her body to know it.

The rest of her, every inch, was emblazoned in his memory.

Her breasts. The delicacy of their weight in his palms. The pale pink of her nipples. The way they pebbled when he caressed them, and the taste of them against his tongue.

His gaze drifted lower.

She didn't look pregnant, although…yes. He saw it now. That slight convexity to her belly beneath the shirt. How would that gentle roundness feel under his hand as he moved it down to the heat between her thighs…?

"Caleb?"

He looked up.

Did she know what he was thinking, what he was reliving, what he wanted now, had wanted all these past weeks?

Every muscle in his body came alive on one hot, sharp rush of sensation.

He stood up, walked to the window, jammed his hands into his trouser pockets and stood staring out at the ugly street while he fought for control.

This was not the time to get sidetracked.

She'd been in the john long enough for him to have come up with a plan, one he could easily implement.

For a couple of minutes, he'd considered not handling the details himself. A lawyer who represented himself had a fool for a client. That was what people said.

But this was straightforward. Simple. He couldn't find much about it she would object to, and that was a plus. Besides, even if she objected, it was how things were going to be.

The law, and logic, were on his side.

He inhaled, hard. Exhaled the same way. Put on his courtroom face. Then he turned and found that she was on her feet, too. He frowned, jerked his head toward the chair.

"Sit down."

Her eyebrows rose. He couldn't blame her. He sounded like a drill sergeant.

"Sorry." He forced a smile. "I only meant that we might as well be comfortable while we discuss our, ah, our—"

"Situation," she said. "Isn't that what you called it?"

He was losing ground and he hadn't even started talking. Why was she standing there, arms folded? Why didn't she sit down? Maybe she was waiting for him.

Okay. He went back to the couch. Sat on the middle cushion. A second went by. Then she settled into the chair again.

"Look, Caleb, I know you weren't expecting—"

"Sage, the thing is, I hadn't expected—"

They spoke at the same time. "You first," he said.

She nodded.

"I don't mean to sound hostile. In fact—in fact, I know I owe you an apology."

She licked her lips. Nerves, he knew, but it was a disconcerting sight, that kitten-pink tongue moistening a strip of flesh he knew was honeyed and tender.

Hell.

He shot to his feet again. Took as no-nonsense a stroll as a man could take through a room the size of a shoebox.

"Yes," he said briskly, "you do. You should have told me the truth right away, but I'm willing to forgive you."

"How nice of you."

So much for apologies. Still, he knew he deserved it. He sounded ridiculous, but no way was he going to admit that.

"My point is, we have—we have a problem for which we need a solution."

He almost winced at the sound of his own words, so stodgy, so formal, so pathetically inadequate.

Sage did more than wince. She fixed him with a look he could only think of as lethal.

"I am," she said, "going to have this baby!"

"You're going to…?" Caleb grimaced. "Did you think I was going to ask you not to?"

"Just so we have that straight."

She was giving him the full treatment now. Icy glare. Raised chin. Folded arms.

"Of course you're going to have this baby." He ran his hand through his hair. "That's what I want to discuss. The baby. You. Me. How we're going to handle this."

She relented, but barely.

"I started to tell you before… I've made plans. Tentative ones, but—"

"I assume you've seen a physician."

"A nurse-practitioner at a clinic. Yes."

"You're not seeing a private ob-gyn?"

There was something in his tone she didn't like. She didn't like the fact that he was standing and she was sitting, either. Had he done that deliberately, for a psychological advantage?

Sage got to her feet. He was still bigger and taller and more imposing than she ever could be but at least she didn't feel like a supplicant.

"No," she said calmly, "I'm not."

"You will, from now on."

She narrowed her eyes. "Will I," she said flatly.

"And this apartment. You can't stay here."

"Were you listening to me at all? I already said—"

"What about your diet? Are you eating the right things?"

"Gruel and alfalfa sprouts," she said pleasantly. "How about you?"

"We're not talking about me, we're talking about…"

She knew the instant he got it. His face, all those gorgeous hard planes and angles, turned crimson.

"Very amusing," he snapped.

"Look," she said, relenting just a little, "I appreciate your concern but I've done just fine on my own so far, and—"

"When are you moving?"

"Soon."

"Where?"

"I told you. Queens. Long Island, New—"

"New Jersey. Yes, so you said."

"If your point is that I haven't completed my plans yet—"

"You don't have 'plans,' you have ideas. There's a big difference."

"Okay. There's a difference. But—"

"I want plans, not ideas, for the baby."

"*My* baby."

"*Our* baby." He watched her as the words sank in—and realized they weren't only sinking in for her, they were sinking in for him, too.

Her baby.

His baby.

Their baby.

She was carrying his child, and she'd be here and he'd be there, in Texas, a million miles away....

So what?

Distance was nothing, not in today's world. Cell phones. Skype. Instant messaging. And, of course, the Wilde jets, always at his command.

Caleb folded his arms. "Here's what I've decided."

"What *you've* decided?"

"Let me finish."

"Let *me* save you the trouble. I don't want your money."

"Excuse me?"

"I said, I don't want your money. Oh, don't look so shocked. I know where this is going."

He raised an eyebrow. "Really."

"You're going to write a check. And I'm going to sign some papers. At least, that's your plan, but—"

"What kind of papers?"

She blinked. "What?"

"I said, since you seem to know what I'm going to say and do, what kind of papers am I going to ask you to sign?"

"Releases. Whatever they're called. Something that says yes, I've accepted your check and no, I won't bother you in the future, and—"

He moved fast; his hands were clasping her shoulders before she could get out of the way.

"What part of what I said before didn't you understand?"

"Let go of me!"

"Or did you not hear me when I said this was *our* baby."

"I heard you. It's a figure of spee—"

"Dammit," Caleb said furiously, and he pulled her into his arms and kissed her.

What are you doing, Wilde?

The still-rational part of his mind posed the question.

The non-rational part gave up thinking.

Maybe she did, too, because after a second of protest, she went up on her toes, wound her arms around his neck and parted her lips to his.

The kiss was everything he'd remembered.

Hot. Deep. Electric. It made everything else unimportant.

His arms tightened around her.

"I have never stopped wanting you," he whispered.

"I've wanted you every day, every night, every minute—"

He kissed her again. She kissed him back. Then he swung her into his arms and carried her to the bedroom, to the bed where all of this had begun.

He undressed her quickly. No finesse. Not now. Not when it had been so long since he'd held her, naked, against him.

He tore off his own clothes. Everything went flying.

"Caleb," she said, raising her arms to welcome him, and he knelt between her thighs and entered her, hard and fast.

She was ready.

Hot. Wet. Sobbing his name at the fierce pleasure of his possession.

"Too quick," he groaned, "too quick…"

He tried to hold back.

She wouldn't let him.

Because it wasn't too quick.

Not for her.

Not for him.

He clasped her hands. Raised them above her head. Sank into her again. Drew back. Sank in deeper, deeper…

"Caleb," she whispered, and his groan of release joined her cry of fulfillment as they flew off the edge of the world.

It seemed a long time before their breathing returned to normal.

"You okay?" Caleb said softly.

Sage smiled. "Yes."

"The baby…?"

"The baby's fine."

He kissed her. Then he rolled to his side with her safely in his arms.

"You're sure I didn't hurt you?"

She laid her hand against his cheek. "Positive."

Slowly, he trailed his index finger over her lips, down her throat, touched each nipple with feathered strokes.

"You have beautiful breasts, sweetheart."

She blushed. God, he loved that blush, he thought as he kissed his way down her body, to her belly.

And yes, it was ever so gently rounded.

"I just started showing," she said softly, as if she'd read his mind.

Showing, he thought. Her belly. Her womb. His seed, and now, his child.

"It makes you look even more beautiful."

She smiled again. "You think?"

"I know."

"Mmm." She wove her fingers through his hair. "Caleb?"

"Yes?"

"I really meant—I don't want you to think—I mean, I don't want you to feel—"

He silenced her with a kiss.

"This is our baby, Sage. I'm only sorry I wasn't here for you before this."

Her eyes filled with tears.

"Don't cry, sweetheart," he said gruffly. "Please. There's nothing to cry about." He moved over her, looked down into her sweet, sweet face. "We're going to do this together. Understand? There's no more you, no more me. There's only us. Okay?"

"Okay," she whispered, and he bent his head, kissed away her tears, kissed her lips…

"Sage," he said thickly, and she opened her arms to him…

More than that.

She opened her heart.

She awoke alone in the bed.

Her heartbeat stuttered. Was he gone? She reached for her robe…

And smiled, as Caleb entered the room. Oh, her lover was beautiful. His hair was rumpled; he was shirtless and barefoot; his trousers, the top button undone, hung low on his hips.

"Morning, sleepyhead," he said.

She blinked. "Is it really morning?"

He came to the side of the bed, leaned down, caged her within his arms and gave her a coffee-laced kiss.

"Morning, evening, I've no idea." He kissed her again, slowly, tenderly. "I made coffee. And herbal tea."

She smiled. "Perfect."

"Of course, we could skip the coffee and tea and get right to dessert…"

Sage's belly rumbled. Caleb grinned, dropped a quick kiss on her forehead and rose to his full height.

"On second thought, how about breakfast?"

* * *

She made scrambled eggs.

He made toast.

"Too bad you don't have any cheese," he said, peering into the fridge.

"I have cottage cheese."

"Cheese," he said with a dramatic shudder. "Real cheese. You know. Yellow. Sliced. Comes in a package—"

It was Sage's turn to shudder.

"Or hot dogs," he said. "Hot dogs would be perfect."

"Please don't tell me those are your favorite food groups!"

He chuckled, shut the fridge and turned toward her. Damn, she was gorgeous. No makeup. Hair long and loose. Lush body wrapped in a robe that kept coming open.

"Caleb? Packaged cheese and hot dogs are...?"

He cleared his throat.

"Specialties of the house," he said. "Well, Wilde brothers' specialties."

"Oh," she said, and it hit him that she didn't know anything about his family, but there'd be time to tell her more.

Except, there wasn't.

Not when he was in a rush to take her back to bed, to make the most of the hours they had left because he had to be back in Dallas by tomorrow.

Their eyes met.

She said his name. He opened his arms. She went into them.

"Sage," he whispered, and she sighed as he lifted her and carried her back to the bedroom.

He kissed his way down her body, pausing to savor the sweetness of her nipples, her navel, the softness between her thighs.

"My turn," she murmured.

Her hands were cool, her mouth warm, her caresses at first cautious, even delicate, and he realized, on a rush of what he knew was foolish masculine ego, that she had never touched another man as she was touching him.

They kissed endlessly, loving the tastes and textures of each other's lips and tongues until, suddenly, there was no more time to spare. He was hungry for the feel of her closing around him. She was hungry for the feel of him deep inside her.

She wept, and came on a high cry of ecstasy.

He followed seconds later, throwing his head back and calling out her name. Then, he collapsed in her arms, sweat-slicked skin against sweat-slicked skin.

After a long, long time, he rolled to his side, stretched out beside her and laid his hand gently over her belly.

He bent his head, pressed a kiss to where his child lay sleeping. She cupped her hand around the back of his head and fell asleep.

He was too busy thinking, planning, making decisions.

After a while, moving carefully so he wouldn't wake her, Caleb rose, collected his clothes and went into the bathroom. He showered, dressed, then called his pilot on his cell phone, telling him to have the jet ready within the hour.

He went back into the bedroom. Sage was still sleeping and he bent down and kissed her mouth.

She stirred, sighed, opened her eyes and smiled.

"Caleb," she said softly.

He sat down next to her and took her hand.

"I have to go home," he said. "I have a meeting. I can't cancel it."

Her smile tilted. "No. That's okay. I understand."

He lifted her hand to his lips.

"I'll fly back next weekend. We'll find an apartment. A house. I'll contact a Realtor."

"I'll do it."

"Sure. Fine. Just be sure to get something in—"

"I know. Something in a safe neighborhood."

"Yeah, well, absolutely. But what I was going to say was, make sure it's on the park."

"The park?"

"Central Park, if you want to stay in Manhattan. Or, I've been to a couple of really handsome towns in Connecticut... What?"

Sage sat up. The duvet dropped to her waist and Caleb bent his head and kissed her breast.

"No," she said, "you have to listen."

"I'm listening," he said in a husky whisper. "But, luckily for you, ma'am, I'm a multitasker."

She laughed, but it was a quick laugh, and she pushed him gently away.

"Seriously, Caleb, I'm not going to take a place on Fifth Avenue, or in one of those—what'd you call them? One of those 'handsome' towns in Connecticut."

He sat back. "Because?"

"Because," she said patiently, "I can't afford them."

"That's just plain silly. *I* can afford them."

Hell. There it was. The narrowed eyes. The cool look.

"You're not going to support me," she said.

"I'm going to support our child. Did you think I wouldn't? Did you think I'd walk away from my responsibility?"

She sat up a little straighter.

"Helping support our child is one thing but I don't intend to be your 'responsibility.'"

He heard the way she said the word, knew she'd taken it in a way he hadn't meant it.

"Sage. Honey, maybe I'm saying this wrong—"

"No. It's me saying it wrong. What I mean is—thank you for wanting to help."

He drew back. "Do not," he said coldly, "absolutely do not thank me."

"I simply meant—"

"Is that what you think this is about? Me, 'helping' you?"

"I didn't meant it that way. It's just…look, I've been on my own for years. I can take care of—"

"If you take care of my child the way you've taken care of yourself—"

"For your information, I've done just fine taking care of myself."

"Oh, right." Sarcasm frosted each word. "One look at this—this palace is proof of that."

Sage struggled with the duvet, managed to keep it clutched to her like a shield, and rose from the bed.

"You know what? I think it's time you left."

"Yeah. I think so, too." Caleb strode to the door, stopped, spun around and pointed his finger at her. Anger was etched into his face. "I don't know what kind of sorry SOB you think I am, but get this straight. I never walk away from a responsibility."

Sage's eyes glittered with angry tears.

"You already told me that. But this isn't a 'responsibility,' it's a baby."

"Goddammit, of course it's a baby! My baby."

"This child is mine. It's part of me. And if you think you're going to take over where Thomas Caldwell left off—"

Caleb said something ugly. Then he turned on his heel and walked out.

CHAPTER NINE

WHAT did women want?

Men had been asking that question for centuries.

Caleb had debated it for most of his thirty-two years, with his brothers, in college dorms, in Marine barracks, over beers with his fellow spooks at the hush-hush camp tucked into the Virginia mountains where he'd prepped for life at The Agency.

He'd never come up with an answer.

Nobody had.

Travis had summed it up.

"Babes don't know what they want," he'd said. "If you're tender, you're a wuss. If you're tough, you're insensitive. You're never smart enough but you sure as hell can be dumb enough, in which case you're a lost cause."

Thirty thousand feet above flyover country, Caleb grimaced into his tumbler of Scotch.

That's what he was. A lost cause.

"Damn right," he muttered, and he raised his glass and took a long, warming swallow.

This time yesterday, he'd been an attorney representing a client.

Now he was... What?

A man on a tightrope. All he could do was put one foot in front of the other and not look down.

Maybe he really should have listened to that old adage about lawyers being fools if they represented themselves.

Except…

He took another drink.

Except, this wasn't a legal thing. Not yet, anyway, unless Sage decided she wanted to try and move him out of the picture.

"Fat chance she has of accomplishing that," he muttered.

He'd put a child in her womb. That gave him certain rights. He was *not* Thomas Caldwell, demanding access to a kid that wasn't his. He wasn't trying to take her baby from her, he just wanted to assume his role as its father.

What kind of woman would tell a man he couldn't do that?

"Mr. Wilde?"

Caleb looked up. The cabin attendant smiled politely.

"Captain wanted me to tell you there's weather moving into Dallas. Things might get a little rough in a couple of hours."

Things were already rough, Caleb thought, but not in the way she meant.

"Right," he said. "Thanks."

"Can I get you anything? A sandwich, perhaps?"

What, he thought, and spoil the buzz he hoped would accompany this, his second shot of whisky?

"Thank you," he said politely. "I'm fine."

She smiled again and went back to the galley.

Caleb drank a little more of the Scotch.

This was one of those times having an entire jet to himself was one damned fine idea. He could pace, as he had already done; drink, as he was now doing; talk to himself and avoid all contact with humanity except for his pilot, his co-pilot and the cabin attendant.

Now if could only avoid contact with himself.…

But he couldn't. His head was full of nonsense.

He kept going over that last confrontation with Sage, trying to figure out how they'd gone from making love to making war with hardly any time in between.

He kept seeing her face, the anger in her eyes…

The passion in them, only a little while before.

"Dammit," he said, and he put aside the tumbler of Scotch, plucked the satellite phone from its niche, punched in a number, heard Travis say hello.

"It's me," Caleb barked.

"Caleb?"

"Isn't that what I just said?"

"Well, no. What you said was 'it's me,' and I hate to tell you this, dude, but there are probably zillions of me's in this world, and I'd bet I know at least a couple of hundred of them."

"Very funny."

"Yeah, well, we aim to please."

"Is Jake with you?"

"You want to be accurate, I'm with Jake at *El Sueño*. As you'll be, in a little while…or are you calling to say you're not gonna make this meeting?"

"Are you in the ranch office? Switch to speaker phone, okay? But shut the door first."

"Any more instructions?"

Caleb closed his eyes, pinched the bridge of his nose between two fingers.

"Travis."

"Yeah?"

"I want to talk to both of you. And I need to warn you, I'm not in a good mood."

"Nothin' new there, pal. You always were too uptight for your own—"

"Trav. I need—I need advice."

Silence. Then he heard his brother say, "Jake? It's Caleb." He heard him say something else, too, but the words were muffled as if Travis had put his hand over the phone.

A second later, he heard the slightly hollow sound that meant Travis had switched to speaker phone.

"Caleb?"

"Jake?"

"Yes. Caleb, Travis says—"

"I, ah, I want to run something by you. Both of you."

"Sure," Jake said.

"Sure," Travis said.

Caleb said nothing. He wasn't sure how to start, or where to start, or even if he should have made this call.

"Caleb? You there, man?"

He nodded. Cleared his throat. And went for it.

"Say there's a guy. Meets a woman. Spends, you know, spends a night with her.

"Sounds good so far," Travis said, chuckling.

"She's, you know, she's okay. Pretty. Smart. Fun. She's—"

"She's nice," Jake said helpfully.

Caleb shook his head.

"She's more than nice. She's—well, she's special."

Silence again. Then, warily:

Jake: "How special?"

Travis: "*Special* special?"

Caleb got to his feet, walked the length of the airplane.

"Yeah." His voice sounded hoarse and he cleared his throat. Again. "Anyway, he meets her. And then, some time goes by. A couple of months. And he finds out she's—he finds out she's pregnant."

There was no mistaking the sudden, sharp intakes of breath that came over the line.

"Wait a minute," Travis said. "They were together only this one time?"

"Right."

"Not again during those two months?"

"Three. Actually, it was three. And, no, they never saw each other after that night. He had no idea she was pregnant."

"What," Jake said, on a huff of disbelief, "she didn't tell him?"

"No. She couldn't. She, ah, she didn't know his last name, didn't have his address, his phone number…"

"But she claims he knocked her up."

"He didn't 'knock her up,'" Caleb growled. "He made her pregnant."

In Jacob's office on the Wilde ranch, two pairs of eyebrows rose.

"And," Travis said carefully, "and he's sure he's the guy who did it?"

"He's sure."

"Because there's been a paternity test?"

"Listen, I didn't call so you two could run an interrogation, I called for—"

"Advice," Travis said, signaling wildly to Jake for a pen and paper. Jake shoved both at him. *WTF is he talking about?* Travis wrote, to which Jake mouthed back, *What am I, a mind reader?*

Caleb had made his way back up the aisle. He sank into his seat, picked up his drink and finished it.

"Here's the problem," he said. "She doesn't want to do anything he says."

Travis: "The paternity test?"

"Not that."

Jake: "You mean, get rid of the—"

"I mean, move out of the rat trap she lives in. Put herself under the care of a top ob-gyn. Let—let this guy buy her things she needs, let him take care of her and, of course, the kid once it's born."

"Of course," Jake said calmly, and clapped his hand to his head.

"He wants to do the right thing," Travis said, just as calmly, and mimed shooting himself in the temple.

"Exactly. He wants to do the right thing. The logical thing. The responsible thing."

Silence again. Caleb rose, paced a little more. In Wilde's Crossing, Texas, Jacob and Travis rose, paced in opposite directions, shaking their heads whenever their paths crossed.

"So," Travis finally said, "who, uh, who are we talking about here, man?"

"A friend," Caleb said quickly. Too quickly. He winced. "Just some guy I know."

"And," Jake said, "and you, ah, you want our advice?"

"Yes. Because I—I haven't been too helpful."

"What did you suggest he do?"

"That's just it. Nothing she'll accept. Not yet."

His brothers looked at each other and pumped their fists in the air.

"Good," Jake said. "Because, you know, he shouldn't do anything precipitous."

Precipitous? Travis mouthed. Jake glared at him.

"Yeah," Caleb said, "but he has to do something. This is his baby. His woman. I mean, she isn't his woman, not really, but—"

"Here's what I think," Jake said. He sat down at the desk, motioned Travis to do the same. "First of all, he needs to arrange for a paternity test. Then he needs to see a lawyer. Work up the legalities. Like—"

"Like the financial obligation your friend is willing to assume," Travis said. "For the woman. For the kid."

"I told you, she doesn't want—"

"If she really doesn't want money," which we strongly doubt, Jake's roll of the eyes said, "he can set it up as a trust. She taps into it? Fine. She doesn't? That's fine, too."

"It isn't. It's not any kind of solution. What if she doesn't touch it? I would never—my friend would never let her go on living from hand to mouth, or let her raise the child in poverty when it's absolutely, totally, completely unnecessary."

"Hell," Jake said softly.

"Caleb?" Travis cleared his throat. "Do you—does this friend care for her? Or is this about—about being responsible?"

"That's what it's about. Being res—" Silence. Then Caleb said, so softly his brothers both leaned toward the phone, "Of course he cares for her. I told you. She's beautiful. She's bright. She's—she's—"

"Caleb," Jake said, "listen man, what I said before, about not doing anything—"

"—precipitously," Travis said. "You need to think. Come home. We can talk—"

"Talking never solved a problem," Caleb said. "A man needs to take action. You flew 'copters, Jake. Travis, you flew jets. I…hell, never mind what I did. The point is, things start going bad, a man needs to take action, not talk. And this—this is a thing starting to go bad."

"Go bad, how?" Jake said softly.

Caleb didn't answer.

"Caleb," Travis said, "tell us what's going on."

"I did," Caleb said, very calmly.

He did? his brothers mouthed to each other.

"And you guys helped. You helped enormously."

"Caleb," Travis said, "is this about that woman in New York? Dammit, is this about you?"

"Me?" Caleb said with all the indignation he could muster. "You have to be kidding. Would I ever get myself into a mess like this? It's about a friend. I told you. A good friend."

"Who?" Jake demanded.

But Caleb had hung up.

Jake depressed the speaker phone button. For an endless moment, neither he or Travis said anything. Then Jake shook his head.

"Oh, man," he said softly.

Travis nodded. "I couldn't have put it better myself."

"Should we go looking for him?"

"Yes. No. Crap. He sounded okay at the end, didn't he?"

"Yeah. Calm. Very calm."

"So, what do you think?"

"I think his friend is named Caleb."

"Yeah. Dammit. So do I." Jake paused. "What's he's going to do?"

Travis considered. Then he sighed.

"Look, the bad news is, this is Caleb. The good news is, this is Caleb. We know how he works."

"He keeps his emotions close. He never asks for advice."

"He just did."

"No," Jake said, "he didn't. He wanted to lay out the situation so he could find a solution."

Silence. Then Travis said, "So, what now? Do we figure out where he is and go after him?"

"If you guys had done that to me after I left Adoré—I mean, Addison—I'd have beaten the hell out of you. And I sure wouldn't have taken any advice you had to offer."

"You're right," Travis said glumly. "We don't want to push him."

"Exactly. Besides, this is Logic-Man. Remember how we used to call him that when we were kids?"

"Yeah," Travis said, trying his best to sound convinced. "You're right. Logic-Man will definitely not do anything—"

"Precipitous," Jake said, and the brothers flashed each other smiles that only they would have recognized as false.

High above the earth, still hundreds of miles from Dallas, Logic-Man stared out the window at a sky filled with puffy white clouds.

A bed of clouds.

As white, as welcoming as the bed he'd shared with Sage hours before.

Sage.

Those angry tears in her eyes when he walked out—

Tears he could have kissed away.

Tears he could have changed with the words he'd felt filling his heart.

Caleb shot to his feet and went to the cockpit.

"Ted?"

"Yes, Mr. Wilde. I was just going to ask Sally tell you the weather's improved. No need to buckle in or—"

"We're going back."

"Back, sir?"

"To New York. To Kennedy Airport. If you need to file a new flight plan, whatever—"

The pilot smiled.

"No problem, sir. Next stop, Kennedy."

Caleb nodded, returned to his seat, and tried to figure out how to handle the battle that would come next.

By the time they landed, he still didn't have a clue.

What would he say that could possibly convince Sage he only wanted to do what was right?

She was so damn independent. So quick to get ticked off.

He'd phoned the limo company before the plane touched down. They'd have a car for him in an hour.

Wait another hour, to deal with this mess? To hell with that.

He phoned Hertz instead, rented a car.

"Any special model, sir?"

"Whatever you have that's fast."

A long, low, mean-looking sports car was already purring when he climbed into it. The trip to Brooklyn, end-of-the-world Brooklyn, should have taken an hour.

He did it in thirty minutes.

He brought the car to a screeching halt at the curb, right beside a fire hydrant and a couple of kids who looked like they'd stepped out of a reality show about street gangs.

Caleb took out his wallet, extracted two hundred-dollar bills and, tearing them in half, gave a half to each kid.

"The car's still here, untouched, when I come back, you get the rest. Understand?"

The kids grinned and nodded. Caleb went past them, ran up the steps to the front door, pushed it open and raced up the stairs.

Then he was standing outside Sage's apartment.

His heart was banging but it didn't have a thing to do with his gallop up those stairs.

What would he say to her? How could he convince her to stop being so stubborn?

Where was Logic-Man when he needed him?

He took a deep breath.

The logic would come, once he started talking. He was a good talker, especially under pressure. It was one of the reasons for his reputation as a hotshot litigator.

Just do it, he told himself, and he rang the doorbell.

Sage had just come out of the shower.

A shower that had been almost ice-cold.

She'd wrapped herself in her robe, padded, barefoot, to the phone and called the super.

"There's no hot water," she'd said, and he'd yawned and said yeah, he'd see what he could do, which she knew pretty much meant he wouldn't do anything and God, that made her angry and she unloaded on him with everything she had.

It wouldn't change anything about the hot water, but she figured it was better than being in tears, especially since that was how she'd spent most of the past few hours.

The super was collateral damage.

Caleb was the real target.

Didn't he understand that she didn't need what he'd offered? His financial support?

She'd provide for her child *and* herself, thank you very much.

What she'd wanted from him, what she'd hoped for from him—

The doorbell rang.

So much for the super not doing anything.

Sage looked down at herself. Robe. Bare feet. Wet hair flopping in her face. Not a fashion plate but who cared? Mr. Del Gatto wasn't a fashion plate, either, not when he wore jeans that gave the world a view it couldn't possibly want whenever he squatted under the sink.

The bell rang again. A fist pounded on the door.

"Dammit," she heard Caleb roar, "open this door!"

Sage had always thought phrases like the blood draining from somebody's head were just examples of overblown prose, but she could feel the blood draining from hers.

Caleb had come back.

"Sage!" The door shook under the pounding of his fist. "Open—the—door!"

She hesitated. Then she took a steadying breath, went to the door, undid the endless locks and saw him standing there, big and hard-looking and angry as hell.

Her eyes narrowed.

What did he have to be angry about?

"What are you doing here?"

He glared at her. She was a mess. Wet, stringy hair. That same old bathrobe. Bare feet...

Rage, more potent than any he'd ever known, swept through him.

"How come this door doesn't have a peephole?"

"I don't know," she said coldly. "You'd have to ask the manufacturer."

"It's ridiculous to have to open a door before seeing who's standing outside it."

Sage folded her arms.

"Thank you for that report from Consumer Complaints. Is that why you came back? To discuss doors?"

"No. Of course not. I—I—" He swallowed hard. His anger was receding; something was moving in to take its place but he wasn't sure what it was, except that it scared the hell out of him. "Sage. We need to talk."

"Try another line, Caleb. I'm all talked out."

"We need to talk sensibly."

She opened her mouth, then closed it. Okay. He was right. They'd done some shouting but little talking and they did, after all, have a shared interest here.

"Five minutes," she said coolly, and opened the door wider.

Caleb stepped over the threshold and shut the door after him.

"Okay." He paused, searched for the right words. "For starters, about the financial thing—"

"I'm not going to talk about that again."

"Fine," he said gruffly. "Don't talk. Just listen. I want to take care of you. Is that so terrible?"

"I don't need anyone to take care of me."

"Maybe not," Caleb said. "Maybe it's just me. Maybe taking care of you is what *I* need…"

Dammit, he thought, and he forgot logic, forgot everything except what he felt for the woman standing in front of him, so strong and beautiful she made his soul ache.

He said something rough, pulled her into his arms and kissed her, hard at first and then with heart-stopping tenderness.

"Don't," she said, "oh God, Caleb, don't…"

It was a protest without meaning because she was kissing him back, the salty taste of her tears on his lips and hers.

He held her closer; the race of their hearts merged.

"Sage," he said thickly, "I'm sorry, sweetheart. I didn't mean to say anything to hurt you." He cupped her face, looked into her eyes. "This isn't about financial responsibility," he said. "It's about us. You. Me. The baby we made together."

"You're a good man, Caleb Wilde. I know that you want to do the right thing—"

"I want more than that. I want the real thing." He brushed his lips over hers. "I want us to be a family."

"What are you saying, Caleb?"

"Sage." He took a steadying breath. "Marry me. Be my wife."

"No," she said, "no, that's crazy—"

"Listen to me, honey. We get along fine."

"Except when we're shouting at each other."

"Except then," he admitted, "but it's only because you're as stubborn as I am."

Was that a smile? A hint of one?

"We respect each other," Caleb continued. "We're good together, in bed and out." He put his hand over her belly. "And we're having a child," he added softly. "Seems to me those are decent, solid things to build a marriage on."

Sage stared into her lover's eyes. He was right; those were solid things to build a marriage on. The world was filled with people who married for far less.

Except, she wanted more.

Tears rolled down her face.

She wanted his love.

His heart.

She wanted the joy of knowing Caleb would bring her into his life even if she weren't carrying his child...

Because she loved him.

She loved this honorable, kind, decent, arrogant, impossible man—

"Sage." He wiped her tears away with his thumbs. "I'll make you happy. I swear it."

She made a sound that might have been a laugh, but Caleb figured that wasn't possible because her tears were coming even faster—

Which only proved how right he was about men not understanding women because even as he figured she was going to turn him down, she smiled through that teary deluge, rose on her toes, touched his lips with hers and said, "Yes."

CHAPTER TEN

SAGE had been born in a small town in Indiana.

The press called that part of the States the American heartland. Meteorologists called it Tornado Alley, but she'd been lucky.

Though tornadoes had touched down only miles from the small frame house she'd grown up in, none had come close enough to sweep her away.

Now, one had. Except, this force of nature wasn't a storm. It was a man named Caleb Wilde.

What happened after a woman accepted a proposal of marriage? Sage had seen enough movies to hazard a guess.

Kisses. Laughter. Incandescent joy.

Okay. She hadn't actually expected that. Caleb's proposal, while tender, had been based on honor. On principle. On doing the right thing.

Still, it would have been nice if the moment of tenderness had lasted just a little longer, if he hadn't gone from concentrating on her to concentrating on his phone.

A quick kiss. A smile. Then he'd stepped back, pulled the phone from his pocket and turned into someone she didn't know...

But then, she didn't know Caleb Wilde at all.

Right now, he was all business, reading, then answering what she assumed was a series of text messages. When he'd finished with them, he made a couple of quick voice calls that consisted mostly of terse commands.

And just when she'd decided he'd forgotten she was in the room, he looked up, saw her, and gave one more terse command, this time to her.

"Pack," he said. Then he turned his back. "Ted," he said crisply, "how soon can you—"

"Why?"

"Hang on, Ted." He smiled politely at Sage. "Why, what?"

"Why did you tell me to pack?"

"So we can get out of here ASAP."

"Where are we going?"

He gave her a long look. Then he spoke into the phone again, told Ted that he'd see him in an hour, and ended the call.

"We're going to the airport," he said. "You don't need much. A change of clothes, perhaps. Toothbrush, comb… although, come to think of it—"

"What are you talking about?"

"What you'll need. Or what you won't need. The bathroom on the plane is fully stocked. Toothbrushes. Shampoo. What I'd guess you'd call toiletries—"

"Are you deliberately playing stupid? What airport? What plane? Did you actually think you could order me to do something without explaining what that something is all about?"

She'd surprised him. It showed on his face. Apparently, not many people spoke back to Caleb Wilde.

A couple of seconds went by; she could almost see him deciding how best to handle what surely was his idea of mutiny.

Finally, he nodded, even managed a smile.

"I suppose I should explain."

"An excellent plan."

"We're flying to Texas."

"We, as in you and this guy, Ted?"

"Ted is my pilot."

"*Your* pilot. As in the pilot of your plane."

"Right."

His own plane. His own pilot. And how, exactly, did that involve...

Oh, God!

"Wait a minute. Do you think I'm going somewhere with you?"

"Of course. To Texas." He paused. "You have a problem with that?"

She stared at him. "You're the one with the problem," she said coolly. "Because I am not going anywhere."

"Look, I don't have time to argue. I have to get back to Dallas."

Her eyes narrowed. "Nobody's stopping you."

"Dammit, Sage..." His phone rang. He ignored it, but it kept ringing. Finally he muttered something, snatched the phone from his pocket and glanced at the screen.

"Caleb," she said, "listen to me—"

He held up his hand.

"Yes," he said into the phone, "that's correct. Call my office. My P.A. will..."

He began pacing the room.

Sage watched him. She tried hard to keep a cool expression on her face but her heart was pounding.

Texas? He expected her to go to Texas? Today? Tonight? She'd all but lost track of time.

Texas, when she'd never been further south than New Jersey? When she had a life here? When she hardly knew the first thing about Caleb or his family or—or—

But she'd promised to marry him...

Obviously, she'd made a mistake.

"Caleb," she said sharply, "Caleb, listen to—"

That hand lifted again.

It was such an imperious gesture. Did he hope she'd not only obey his commands but curtsy, too?

A hot ball of anger lodged in her chest. It was a much safer emotion than the quick lick of terror and she embraced it, let it flood her senses as she stepped into the path he seemed determined to wear into the thin carpet.

He stopped dead, eyebrows raised.

"Hang up," she said between her teeth.

If his eyebrows lifted any higher they would disappear into his hair.

"I mean it, Caleb. Hang. Up. The. Phone!"

He looked at her as if she were a new species, one he'd never seen before.

"I'll call you back," he snapped. Then he tossed the phone on a chair, folded his arms, and glared at her.

"Well?"

"Remember what I said about Thomas Caldwell?"

"I remember. And I resent the hell out of—"

"I don't care what you resent. I am not going to hop from the frying pan into the fire."

Caleb's eyes blazed.

"I am not Caldwell," he said flatly. "Got that straight?"

"The principle's the same."

"The hell it is!"

"You cannot make decisions for me and about me, without consulting me."

"That's not what I'm doing."

"Isn't it?"

"No. Yes. I mean, dammit…" He hissed out a breath, pivoted on his heel, turned to face her again. "Look," he said in a tone so disgustingly, glibly reassuring it made her teeth ache, "I'm simply trying to expedite things."

"By dragging me to Dallas."

"It's where I live. Where I practice law. I have commitments…"

"You have a life in Dallas."

"Yes. Exactly. And—"

"And I have one here. You can't simply—you can't simply—"

"Did you think we were going to do this long distance? You in New York? Me in Texas? Did you think I was going to be a—a part-time husband and father?" His mouth twisted. "I don't know what your childhood was like but I grew up with one of those."

"I didn't grow up with any, and I—and I—"

"And you what? Grew up just fine anyway?" He took a step toward her, came so close she had to tilt her head back to meet his angry eyes. "Maybe you did. I sure didn't. And I'm not about to do the same thing to a child of mine."

Sage opened her mouth, then shut it. She wasn't going to lie to him or to herself.

"You're right," she finally said, "I didn't, either. Grow up just fine, I mean. But—"

"But, what? Don't you want more for our child? I sure as hell do."

Sage stared at him.

Everything he'd said made sense.

Of course she wanted a different life for her child. For their child. But—but—

She sank down on the sofa.

This was all happening too fast. It was all too new. She'd only just got used to being pregnant and now there was a man in her life. Not just a man. A powerful, demanding man, intent on doing the right thing because it was, well, right, which was wonderful, it was amazing...

Except, what she wanted from him was—was—

"Sage." He squatted down beside her. "Sage, look at me."

She shook her head.

She didn't want to look at him, not when his voice was suddenly so soft, when he was taking her hands in his and bringing them to his lips.

"Sweetheart," he said, and she looked into his eyes and

saw all the things a woman could possibly hope for in their indigo depths.

"Caleb." Her voice broke. "it's—it's too much. It's—it's like getting on what's supposed to be an easy ride at the amusement park and—and having it turn into the world's biggest, baddest, fastest roller coaster."

He laughed softly.

"I've been called a lot of things, honey, but the biggest, baddest, fastest roller coaster is a first."

She laughed, too, but he knew she was trying not to cry, and it tore him in pieces to see it.

"I'm sorry," he said. "I know I should give you more time. In the best of all worlds, we'd do this slowly. Get to know each other. Go out to dinner. Take in a couple of movies, me yawning through a chick flick, you rolling your eyes while Tom Cruise risks his neck in the hundredth version of *Mission Impossible*."

Her eyes still glittered but she smiled. Caleb smiled back at her.

"We'd go to the park. The museums. The zoo." Ah, hell. Two perfect tears were rolling down her cheeks. "Not the zoo, huh?" he said softly, wiping away the tears with his thumbs.

"I don't like keeping animals in cages," she said, and she thought, wasn't this stupid? That she should be weeping?

"See? We have something in common already. Neither do I." His smile tilted. "I'd spend a few days here, fly to Dallas, fly back next weekend. After a couple of weeks, I'd take you home with me. Show you my city. Show you *El Sueño*—"

"What's *El Sueño?*"

"The Dream. The family ranch."

"A ranch." She swiped the back of her hand over her nose. "A real ranch?"

Caleb thought of the half a million rich acres that made up *El Sueño*. He thought of the stables. The barns. The paddocks. The prize-winning stallions, the mares that dropped prize foals in late winter and early spring, the oil wells...

"Yes," he said gently. "It's a real ranch." He took a pristine white handkerchief from his pocket and folded it around her nose. "Go on, honey. Blow." She did, and he took away the handkerchief, slipped his arms around her, drew her against him, one hand in the center of her back, the other stroking her hair. "You'll like *El Sueño,* Sage. And my family."

"Your family," she whispered, "I almost forgot about them. Two brothers. Three sisters."

"And my father."

"The rancher, right?"

Caleb hesitated. How would she deal with his way of life? She could handle it, he was sure of that. But would she want to? There was so much she didn't know...

Might as well get it over with, he decided, and he drew back a little and looked into her eyes.

"Here's the rundown. One sister, Lissa, lives on the west coast—she's a cooking nut but don't ever tell her I called her that."

Another smile. He was batting one hundred.

"Em and Jaimie live right here, in New York. Em's into music. Jaimie is trying to make it as a designer."

"They sound nice."

"They are. You'll like them, and they'll like you."

"And your brothers? Do they live in Texas, like you?"

He nodded.

"Jake runs *El Sueño* and his own place, too. His wife is terrific. She's a lawyer, like me. That just leaves Travis." Caleb grinned. "He's this hotshot financial whiz."

"And your father? If your brother runs the ranch, what does he do?"

Caleb hesitated. "Our father is—he's an army man."

"Ah. A soldier."

"A general, honey. General John Hamilton Wilde."

Sage jerked back in his arms. "A general?"

"Four stars," Caleb said solemnly. "Just to put you completely at ease."

She saw the laughter in his eyes, saw compassion, too, and suddenly she was willing to admit her anger had been terror in disguise.

"It's going to be hard," she said. "Isn't it?"

A muscle knotted in Caleb's jaw. She was looking at him the same way she'd looked at him the night they'd met, equal parts trust and fear in her lovely face.

"Challenging, maybe." He drew her closer. "But we'll be fine, Sage. What we're doing is right. For the baby. And for us." He hesitated. "What I said before. About us being good together. It's—it's more than that. I, ah, I care for you. You matter to me. You—you—"

There were words swimming around in his head, but none that made sense, which meant it was safer to kiss her than to try and say anything more.

"I've been a fool," he said gruffly. "I asked you to marry me, and then I tried to go on as if nothing had changed."

She nodded. "I understand. It's—it's a huge thing we're doing. Getting married. Raising our child together."

"Yeah. It is. But it's the right thing, and we both know it." He stroked her hair back from her face. "I don't want to take charge of your life, Sage. I only want to—to find the best way to make this work."

Sage sighed. His arms tightened around her; she put her head on his shoulder and leaned into him, into all that strong, protective, masculine warmth.

"It's hard for me," she said softly, "hard to, you know, walk away from everything familiar."

He nodded. Told himself the way to do this was to keep it light.

"I know. Heck, who would willingly give up this magnificent apartment?"

She drew back a little, her palms against his chest, and looked at him.

"And your neighbors. That pair of charming gentlemen I was fortunate enough to meet, for instance. I can only imagine how you'll miss them."

That won him a tiny smile.

"And the view. The ambience. The furnishings."

"Hey," she said, "this is vintage stuff."

"Especially that sofa. It must date back fifty years."

"Seventy-five," she said, "according to the Salvation Army, but who's counting?"

Caleb grinned. "Have we left anything out?"

Her smile flickered to life again.

"Only the mouse that lives behind the kitchen sink."

"Ah. You didn't tell me you had a pet."

She laughed. Really laughed. He grinned, and then he rose to his feet and brought her to her feet, too. His grin faded; his eyes turned so dark a blue they were almost black.

"We're going to be okay," he said softly. "You'll see."

"It's just... I grew up poor, Caleb. In a small town. Just the opposite from you."

"You haven't seen Wilde's Crossing," he said with a quick smile. "Talk about small—"

"You know what I mean. We come from such different backgrounds..."

"We do," he said gravely. "Like Jake and Addison. Different as night and day, but what can you expect when a Texan marries a Yankee?"

That won him another smile.

"Seriously, Addison had to make so many changes—"

"Not Jake?"

"Well, some—but mostly, see, easterners, *northerners,* talk funny."

Another smile. Bigger this time.

"We do, huh?"

"And your eating habits…"

"Don't tell me she had to learn to like grits!"

"Of course, but mostly… Remember me looking for cheese and hot dogs?"

"Uh-huh."

It was a wary "uh-huh," but she was smiling again, which was exactly what he'd wanted.

"Well, one very important thing Wilde brides have to do is learn to appreciate a couple of old family recipes."

"Biscuits and yams?"

Caleb grinned.

"Fried cheese and fried hot dogs."

"Oh, yuck!"

"Topped off by charred marshmallows."

"Caleb Wilde. This is a joke, right?"

"Old family recipes," he said gravely "Wilde brothers' recipes, anyway, from our misspent youth. Jake's the sandwich guy. Travis is the hot-dog king. And I," he said with great modesty, "am the marshmallow connoisseur."

Sage began to laugh. He felt that laugh rocket through him, straight down to his toes, and he gathered her close and held her tightly to him.

"I promise," he said softly. "We'll be fine."

"I hope so," she whispered, her breath warm against his throat."

"We will be. You'll see." He lifted her face to his and looked deep into her eyes. "Trust me, sweetheart. Okay?"

Sage hesitated. Trust him. Trust this man who had broken her heart, then put all the pieces of it together again…

"Sage? Will you trust me?"

She took a deep breath.

"Yes," she whispered, and knew she had gone from opening her heart to giving it to him, with no restrictions.

* * *

He assured her they weren't going to Dallas, then asked her to go into the bedroom and pack.

"It's a surprise," he said, when she started to ask him the reason. "Trust me, remember?"

Once the door shut after her, Caleb let out a long breath.

The truth was, he needed a couple of minutes alone.

She was scared. Hell, so was he.

He'd come to New York prepared to make quick work of a woman who'd humiliated him.

Instead, he'd discovered he'd made a terrible error in judgment. About her. About a lot of things. And he'd—he'd become taken with her. Such an old-fashioned word but how else to describe what he felt?

If that wasn't enough to terrify a man, he couldn't imagine what was.

His phone rang.

Caleb ignored it.

Don't do anything precipitous, his brothers had said, but how else to deal with this situation except to move quickly?

He didn't regret his decision.

Sage was everything a man could want. Everything *he* could want.

She was a woman a man could love.

The breath damned near seized in his lungs. Was that what this was all about? Was he—was he—

His phone rang again, this time giving the demented beeps that meant he had a text message. He grabbed the thing as if it were a lifeline.

The message shot him straight back to reality.

It was from Thomas Caldwell.

Is it true you canceled that test, Wilde? I demand an immediate explanation. Repeat, an immediate explanation.

Caleb bit back a groan.

How could he have let things slip so badly? He'd have to contact Caldwell…

But not right now.

He had other calls to make first.

He'd used his law practice as the reason he had to go back to Dallas but the truth was, it had just been an excuse.

His calendar was clear for the next week. He had a handful of client meetings, nothing major, especially since he now had a partner who could stand in for him.

Jake's wife. Addison, or Adoré, as nobody was supposed to know Jake called her—except all of them did—was one fine lawyer.

Caleb almost hit the speed-dial button that would have connected him to his office, but didn't.

Why phone, when you could text and head off questions you weren't ready to answer?

There would be a lot to tell his family, and soon, but first, he and Sage needed some time to themselves.

Hung up here, he texted. Can you handle things for a week?

Addison texted right back.

Sure. Not a problem. And then she added, Is everything okay? which could have been just a general question or a more specific one, meaning Jake had maybe told her about the phone call he and Travis had with their brother.

It didn't matter.

The only appropriate answer was Everything's great, see you soon.

What next?

Right. A call to his pilot.

"Take a few days off," he told Ted. "I'll be in touch when I need you."

The last call was the most important.

He phoned his hotel, a tower of glass that overlooked Central Park. He liked the place; it was modern, elegant, laid-back. The concierge knew him well; he took the same suite whenever he was in town.

Now he told him that he'd want the suite for another week, and he added a few important instructions.

"I'll attend to it at once, Mr. Wilde," the man said. Caleb could almost hear the smile in his voice.

He glanced at his watch. He could get back to Caldwell…

"Caleb?"

Sage's voice was soft.

Caleb sprang to his feet, turned toward the bedroom—and felt his throat constrict.

She'd changed into a dress and sandals. The dress was a shade of blue that came as close to matching her eyes as anything that wasn't the sky ever could. It was simple—thin straps, a full skirt that skimmed her knees. The shoes were simple, too, with skinny high heels and an amalgam of straps. He'd have said their color was tan but he knew enough about women to be pretty sure the right name was far more fanciful.

Her hair was pulled back, sort of knotted on top of her head, and his hands itched to go to her, undo that knot, undo what looked like half a dozen buttons and leave her in just those sexy shoes and whatever she had on under the dress…

"What?" she said with a puzzled smile.

What, indeed.

"You're so beautiful you make my heart ache," he said in a rough voice as he drew her into his arms.

Amazing, that this proud, incredible woman was his. His to care for. To protect. To cherish. To share his life with.

Sage was his.

And he…

He was hers.

CHAPTER ELEVEN

CALEB'S rental car was where he'd left it, the two kids standing next to it with zealous determination in their eyes.

He dug out the halves of the hundred-dollar bills, gave one to each boy.

"Excellent job," he said, and then he thought, what the hell, and gave each kid a hundred bucks more.

It wasn't every day a man asked a woman to marry him.

Marriage.

"Wow," he said softly, as he pulled away from the curb.

"Wow, what?" Sage said.

Caleb reached for her hand and brought it to his lips.

"Just 'wow,'" he said with a quick smile.

"As in, 'Wow, this is all happening so fast'?"

"Yes," he said, because it was senseless not to admit it. "But I told you, we're going to be fine."

"So," she said, trying for a smile. "You're one of those the-glass-is-half-full people."

"Actually, I'm a pragmatist." He laced his fingers through hers, lay their entwined hands over the gearshift. "And that's how I know we'll be fine. It's not as if we're going into this blind. We know who we are and what we're doing. We've been honest with each other, and honesty's the basis of any successful relationship."

"Wow, all over again," Sage said softly.

He grinned. "Sorry. I didn't mean to sound like Dr. Phil."

He pulled to a stop at a red light and looked at her. "I know we're bound to hit some bumps in the road during the next few weeks. You have to tell me if I don't notice."

She nodded. "And you'll do the same with me."

"Hey," he said lightly, "honesty and trust. How can we lose?"

She smiled. "In that case…"

"Yes?"

"Are you ever going to tell me where we're going?"

"I wanted to surprise you."

"Everything that's happening is a surprise."

She was right. And look at how his last attempt at a surprise, the abortive flight to Dallas, had turned out. Maybe surprising her wasn't the way to go.

"To my hotel. *My* hotel, not that fancy funeral parlor Caldwell chose for our meeting."

"Wasn't it awful? Like a set for *The Addams Family*."

"That old TV series. Yeah."

"The Broadway show. I was in it."

The light went to green; he gunned the engine and the car shot forward.

"Time for another 'wow,'" he said, smiling at her.

"Not really. I had three whole lines in the first act."

"Acting's a tough profession, huh?"

"Uh-huh. I've done off-Broadway. And a lot of off-off Broadway. And a lot, a *lot,* of commercials."

"I don't know much about acting." He glanced at her. "But there's lots of theater in Dallas."

"I don't know Texas at all."

"Well, you will. Soon. It's not as big as New York but—"

She squeezed his hand. "It'll be okay," she said softly.

"Yes," he said gruffly, "it will. I'll show you all my favorite haunts. And if you don't like my condo, we'll buy something else."

"Is that where you live? I thought you lived on *El—El—*"

"*El Sueño*. It's the family ranch and I do spend some time there but I'm in Dallas most of the week." He glanced at her. "Heck. Who wants to raise a kid in a city high-rise? We'll look for a house. Maybe a ranch. Outside Dallas. Even in Wilde's Crossing. Would you like that?"

She hesitated. "I don't—I don't know what to say, Caleb. It's all so new..."

"Hey." He let go of her hand, touched her cheek, her hair, and silently cursed himself for a fool. He was trying to make her happy but he was loading too much on her slender shoulders. Honesty and trust were great, but some things were better put aside until the moment was right. "There's no rush for any of this, Sage. We'll take things one day at a time, okay?"

"Thank you," she said softly. "For understanding that this is—that it's—" She swallowed. "I guess I'm one of those people who has to ease into new situations, you know? I mean, it took me a while to figure out New York."

He knew she was trying to make him feel better, so he told her it had taken him a while, too.

"I mean, it's confusing. What's with the five boroughs thing? Only Manhattan is New York."

"Is that an attack on Brooklyn, Mr. Wilde?"

"Uh-oh."

"Uh-oh, indeed," she said, laughing.

It was good, hearing her laugh. Definitely, he'd have to remember not to layer too many things on her for a while.

"Anyway, you've got it wrong."

He raised his eyebrows. "Me? Get something wrong? Impossible."

"Manhattan is New York but it's really *the city*. All the other boroughs are New York, too, but they aren't *the city*." She rolled her eyes. "Clear as mud, right?"

"No. Actually, it's as succinct a description as I ever heard."

They rode in easy silence for a few minutes before Sage turned toward him again.

"Caleb?"

"Yes?"

"When are we going to leave here? For Dallas, I mean? I know you have to get back to the real world, sooner or later."

He cleared his throat. "Well, I thought we'd stay here the rest of the week…"

"Oh," she said.

There was a world of weight in the one soft word. Caleb glanced at her. She was sitting back in her seat, hands folded in her lap, staring straight out the windshield.

"You're worried about meeting my family," he said softly. "Trust me, honey. They'll be surprised, but they'll be happy for me. For us."

Sage nodded. She wanted to believe that, wanted to trust him—she *was* trusting him, not just with her future but with her heart. And that was part of the problem, part of what made all that was happening so dangerous…

"Here we are."

She looked up. They'd pulled to the curb with Central Park to one side, a tall building to the other.

Caleb undid his seat belt, reached over and undid hers.

"Such a long face," he said softly. "That's not a way to start the first week of our lives together."

She looked at him. "That's a very nice thing to say."

He grinned. She loved that grin. Part arrogance, part mischief, completely and heart-stoppingly male.

"What? You think we legal eagles can only speak tort?"

Sage laughed. "What I think is that you're full of surprises."

"Only good ones," he said, as he took her in his arms and kissed her.

"Ahem. Sir? Madam?"

A liveried doorman stood beside the car, trying his best not to smile.

Sage blushed. Caleb grinned.

"I'll need the valet to take my car," he said.

"Of course, sir."

The doorman reached for the door handle, which gave Caleb enough time to lean in and give Sage one last, quick kiss.

"Stop that," she whispered, but her cheeks were rosy, her eyes were bright, and she was laughing.

Caleb stepped from the car, whistling, and tossed the keys to the uniformed kid who'd just shown up. Sage thanked the doorman as he offered her his hand and courteously helped her onto the sidewalk.

"Welcome to Hotel New York," he said with a polite smile.

Caleb slid his arm around her waist.

"Should we tell him he has it wrong?" he whispered, his lips against her ear.

Sage looked up at her lover's smiling face, and felt her heart flood with emotion.

When could she tell him what he meant to her?

Or was there such a thing as taking honesty a step too far?

His suite was beautiful.

Big. Bright. Airy.

"No funerals allowed here," Caleb said solemnly.

The sitting-room windows overlooked Central Park, as did those in the bedroom. A small formal dining room opened just off the sitting room; a master bath Sage figured was almost the size of her entire apartment opened off the bedroom.

But what made her catch her breath on a long "ooh" of delight were the flowers.

Roses and tulips, orchids and daisies, varieties she couldn't possibly have named, standing tall and elegant in crystal vases, nodding gracefully in white ceramic bowls, drooping like elegant ballerinas in pale blue pottery jugs.

"Oh, Caleb," she said, her face glowing with pleasure. "Did you arrange for this?"

Was he blushing? He hadn't even known he could blush, but he could feel the heat rising into his face.

"Do you like them?" he said, his voice gruff. "I wasn't sure what kinds of flowers you liked best, so—"

She flung herself into his arms.

He held her close. Closer still. Buried his face in her hair and felt—felt his eyes blur.

What was happening to him? Because something definitely was. What had started as The Right Thing was turning into something more.

"I wanted this day, this night, to be special for you," he said.

She looked up, her eyes brilliant with tears.

"You're what's special," she said, "you, Caleb, you—"

He kissed her. Kissed her again. Her tears became sighs, her sighs became moans, and he did what he'd longed to do back in her apartment.

Took the pins from her hair.

Took off her dress.

Helped her step free of it as it pooled at her feet.

She was wearing a pale blue lace bra and panties. And those impossibly high, impossibly sexy heels.

She was beautiful.

And she was his.

He took her in his arms. Kissed her, searched out the sweetness of her mouth, groaned as she undid his belt, his fly, slipped her hand inside and found his heat, his hardness, his hunger.

For her. Only for her. Because she was his. His...

Caleb yanked his shirt over his head, kicked off his shoes, pulled off the rest of his clothing. Then he swung Sage into his arms, carried her to the bedroom and made love to her until she came apart beneath him.

He watched her face as it happened, heard her sob his name, and knew that his life had changed, not just because of the baby they'd created together, but because of Sage.

Because he'd found her.

Because—because—

He gave up thinking.

And shattered with her.

There was a small fridge in an alcove just off the dining room.

Wrapped in one of the luxurious white robes the hotel had provided, Sage rummaged within it, said a triumphant "Ta da!" and turned toward Caleb with a small platter of cheeses in one hand and a bowl of big, ripe strawberries in the other.

He grinned, extracted the cork from a bottle of champagne.

"Non-alcoholic," he said, as he poured the bubbly stuff into two flutes. "And now… Dinner in bed, madame?"

"An excellent suggestion, sir."

They took their loot into the bedroom and climbed onto the bed, leaned back against the stacked pillows and feasted.

Sage said the pseudo-champagne was lovely.

Caleb rolled his eyes and said it was, for certain, preferable to herbal tea.

The cheeses were delicious. The berries were sweet and when some of the juice dribbled over her lips, Sage said they needed napkins.

Caleb said they didn't, and proved it by licking the juice from her lips, her throat, her breasts.

She gave a little "mmm" of pleasure, a soft moan when he drew her nipple into his mouth.

"Still want that napkin?" he growled against her soft flesh.

"I'm not sure," she said breathlessly. "You'll just have to convince me—"

"Put your glass down."

"Why?" she said, in a sexy whisper surely meant to drive him crazy.

Caleb poured a few drops of his drink over her belly, then licked it away.

Sage gasped. Her hand shook.

"That's why," he said.

She put her glass on the table. He let some more of the liquid drip on her. Lower. And lower. Lower still, until he nuzzled her thighs apart.

"Now this," he said thickly, "this is a definite improvement over herbal tea."

Sage whispered his name.

"I love the taste of you here," he said thickly. "And the scent. I love—"

She cried out.

One last taste of her. One last kiss. Then his champagne flute fell, forgotten, to the carpet. He rose up, kissed her mouth and sank into her.

The whirlwind caught them up again, spun them off the edge of the world until he collapsed in her encircling arms.

When their breathing finally slowed, he gathered her close, rolled onto his side holding her, and they tumbled into sleep.

They showered in the enormous glass shower stall.

Sage announced that the bathroom really was twice the size of her entire apartment. And the hot water didn't give out after just a few minutes, a very good thing because it lasted enough for Caleb to say, "Here, let me do that," take the sea sponge from her hand, and bathe her with it.

Every sweet inch of her, from top to bottom.

He dried her, too, with a fluffy white bath sheet as they stood beneath the heat lamps.

She gasped as he dried places that required extra tender

care, as he kissed her and teased her with his mouth, his hands, his fingers.

Then it was her turn to dry him. To tease him. Explore him, until one touch led to another, one kiss to another…

He carried her back to bed. She wrapped her legs around his hips.

"Caleb," she gasped.

"Yes," he groaned, "yes…"

Later, they fell asleep in each other's arms.

When they awoke, the sky was black. Central Park wore the city's fabled skyline like a necklace of diamonds.

"I," Caleb said, "am hungry enough to eat a—"

"Fried cheese sandwich with a fried hot dog on the side?"

He grinned, told her to be careful what she wished for, sat up and reached for the phone.

They put on the terry-cloth robes again. A waiter brought their dinner; Caleb met him at the sitting-room door, thanked him, tipped him extravagantly and said he'd take over from here.

He didn't want to share this night with anyone.

He wheeled the serving cart to the windows. Dragged over a pair of chairs. Sage lifted the silver lids from the plates and platters.

Grilled steaks. Tiny roasted red potatoes. Baby carrots and asparagus slender as toothpicks.

"Where's yours?" she said with wide-eyed innocence. Then she picked up a potato and popped it, whole, into her mouth.

"Good?" Caleb asked.

"No," she said. "But I'll make the sacrifice. I'll eat it all, to save you from food poisoning."

He laughed, leaned over and kissed her.

They ate every morsel, opened another bottle of the not-really-Champagne.

Then Caleb wheeled the cart into the dining room and they settled on the floor in front of the flower-filled fireplace, the last of the fizzy non-wine in their glasses, and leaned back against a big stack of black-and-white pillows.

Caleb drew Sage into the curve of his arm.

She sighed. Then she said, in a deadly serious tone, "Okay, Caleb Wilde, the time has come."

His heart thudded. Was she going to say she'd changed her mind about marrying him?

"I want to know everything about you." She looked at him. "For starters," she said with a smile on her lips, "have you always been a knight?"

He laughed. "Trust me, sweetheart. I've never been that."

Her smile faded; her expression turned serious.

"I do trust you," she said softly. "And I never thought I'd say that to any man."

Caleb kissed her temple. "Want to tell me about it?"

She hesitated. And then she knew that she did, that this was part of what made everything between them special.

That they could be honest and open with each other.

So she sat up straight, scrunched around until she was sitting, cross-legged, facing him.

"I grew up in Indiana," she said, "in a little town in the middle of nowhere."

Just the two of them, she said, she and her mother. And, she said, without any embarrassment or apology, the same direct way she'd said it before, they'd been poor.

It hurt him, to think of her as a kid without the things he'd pretty much taken for granted, but what hurt most was when he realized, as she talked, that her childhood, her teen years, her life in that little town in the middle of nowhere, had been defined more by her mother's bitterness, by the absence of a father, than by poverty.

His own mother had died when he and his brothers were very small but he had warm memories of the woman who'd become their stepmother. And though none of them could ever pretend their relationship with their father had been warm or traditionally loving, at least they'd had a father.

She told him how she'd come to New York with two hundred dollars she'd saved from working at the local diner when she was in high school. How she'd found a flat she'd shared with five other girls.

"Picture it, six women, all fighting for the bathroom," she said, making light of what he knew must have been a tough couple of years.

"Then," she said, "I got a part in a Sandra Bullock movie. I was supposed to just sit near her in a restaurant scene but I ended up with a line to speak."

"And you were great."

"Of course," she said archly. They both smiled. "Seriously, I guess I was okay because I got a few more parts and then my agent snagged me a TV ad." She fluttered her lashes. "I was a talking box of corn flakes."

He laughed, took her hand, kissed each finger and said he'd never look at corn flakes the same way again.

"I met David right after that." Her tone softened. "He was wonderful. Funny. Caring. Smart. He became the big brother I'd never had. Everybody liked him—except for his father. Once David came out, Caldwell disowned him. He wouldn't even take his calls."

Caleb reached for her and drew her into his lap.

"I'm sorry for what I did that night. To David, you know? I shouldn't have—"

"It was okay. Really." She smiled. "David said it was a compliment. See, he was trying out for a part where he was going to play a straight guy so he figured if you didn't think he was gay…" She leaned her head against Caleb's shoulder. "That's enough about me. You're supposed to be telling me about you."

"Well," he said, "let's see…"

What could he tell her? He wasn't a man who liked talking about himself; he knew he'd always held his feelings close, but that was simply the way he was.

Well, he could tell her about his family.

His brothers, first.

He expanded a little on what he'd already said about them, explained that Jake had returned from war a wounded hero, that Travis was fearless, that his sisters were like her.

"Like me?" she said with a pleased smile.

"Yes," he said, because it was true. "They're pretty and smart, feminine as heck but tough as nails when they have to be. So is Jake's Addison." He hugged her. "You're going to fit right in, sweetheart."

"I hope so," she said softly. "And your father? The general?"

"Let's see. Smart. Stuffy. Superior."

"The three Ss," Sage said.

Caleb smiled. "Exactly. And that's all of it."

"No, it isn't."

"It is. Two brothers. Three sisters. One father—"

"You still haven't said a word about you."

He hesitated. Then he figured, okay, why not?

He told her how he'd gone from wanting to be a cop to wanting to be a lawyer. And then, to his amazement, he found himself talking about his five-year detour into intelligence, how he'd been recruited by one of his law-school profs.

"I said thanks, but no thanks. I said I was too much of a maverick to be a spy." He gave a self-deprecating laugh. "I wanted to get a rise out of him but he just said, sure, that was one of the reasons he'd thought I'd be right for the job."

"And you were," Sage said gently.

"For a while. At first, it was exciting. And fulfilling. But, after a while, I knew it wasn't where I wanted to spend the rest of my professional life. I saw things…" His mouth twisted. "Hell, I did things…"

She leaned in. Kissed him

"I bet you never did anything you didn't think was right."

It was true. He hadn't.

That was why he'd left The Agency.

He'd been able to make peace with risking his life, the lives of others, even once or twice implementing the taking of lives, for the security of his country and his people.

But things had begun to change. The rationale for some of his assignments struck him as murky, even specious.

He'd balked. Once. Twice. And he and The Agency had parted ways.

Caleb told Sage about it.

No details—he would always be bound to secrecy—but he wanted her to know everything about him, the good and the not-so-good.

Finally, he fell silent.

And realized he was holding his breath, until she raised her face to his and kissed him.

"Sir Knight," she said softly, and when he shook his head, she kissed him again. "You're the best person I've ever known," she whispered, and his heart swelled with joy.

After a minute, she said, "Does your family—do they know about us?"

"No. Not yet. I'll tell them. Soon. But you got me thinking today. We need some time alone."

"Yes. Thank you for that."

"The thing is, I love my brothers and I'm crazy about my sisters—but they can be a little overwhelming."

"The Wilde Bunch?"

He laughed. "Actually, that's what my brothers and I called ourselves, growing up."

"So, when will you—"

"Soon," he said, and kissed her, and the world went away.

* * *

Morning brought a steady summer rain.

And a problem.

"We have to go back to my apartment," Sage announced as they were finishing breakfast.

"Because?"

"Because you should have told me I'd need more than one dress and a pair of jeans!"

Caleb smirked.

"What?"

"I have plans for today," he said.

"Whatever they are, first I have to get some more—Caleb Wilde, what's with that look?"

Caleb pushed back his chair.

"Up," he said.

Sage tilted her head. "Are we back to one-word commands?"

He leaned down, kissed her and smacked his lips.

"I'm starting to like the taste of herbal tea."

"Nice try, but I still want to know what's going on."

"Get dressed. And you'll see."

She put on the jeans and T-shirt she'd brought. He wore jeans, too, with a white cotton sweater. They went down to the lobby, the doorman whistled up a cab and held a big black umbrella over their heads as he hurried them to it.

Several minutes later, their cab pulled up in front of Saks Fifth Avenue.

"Caleb," Sage said in a warning tone.

"That's my name," he said cheerfully.

"Caleb," she said, as he hustled her through the rain and into the store, "what are we doing here?"

"You can't spend a whole week in one pair of jeans and that blue dress. Of course," he added, in his best I-am-a-lecher tones, "you could spend it naked in bed with me, but the chambermaid has to get in to clean once in a while."

A woman hurrying past them laughed.

Sage swatted him on the arm.

"Keep your voice down," she hissed. "And didn't I tell you that same thing? We have to go to my place so I can get—"

Caleb took her hand and hurried her past silk scarves and handbags and counters of makeup.

"No dilly-dallying," he said briskly. "Not when there's a bunch of people waiting to meet you."

Sage came to a dead stop. "What people?" Understanding rose in her eyes. "If you think I'm going to let you buy—"

He pulled her into his arms and kissed her.

"Caleb, for heaven's sake, not here, in the middle of—"

"Right here. Right now. I'll keep kissing you until you finally say yes, a man can buy a few things for his wife."

"I'm not your wife—"

"Not yet," he said, and kissed her again.

"You're impossible!"

"I'm also very, very determined. What's it going to be? A kissing marathon, or a shopping trip?"

A kissing marathon, she wanted to say. And when he flashed that wicked, sexy grin she loved, she grinned back at him.

"Okay. You win. But only a few things. Necessities."

"I wouldn't have it any other way," Caleb said, lying through his teeth as he led her to the elevators.

It was clear the sales staff had been expecting him. Or a man like him, one who knew precisely what he wanted.

Dresses were, he said, necessities. So were jeans and trousers, skirts and tops, lingerie, shoes and sandals and anything and everything in between.

"Caleb, no," Sage whispered, "it's too much."

"It's not half enough," he answered, loving the pleasure he saw in her eyes as she looked in the mirror, wearing silk and linen and all the things she'd never had before.

Once he'd arranged for all the bags and boxes to be sent to the hotel, they went back down to the first floor.

"Pick out a couple of handbags," he said.

Sage stared at the bewildering assortment.

"There are so many..."

Indeed, and he'd counted on that.

Once she was busy comparing what looked like bowling bags to what had to be sacks, he took the salesclerk aside.

"Keep her busy," he whispered, "for maybe fifteen minutes."

Cartier was just minutes away.

He ran through the rain, found the manager waiting for him with ten beautiful rings laid out on a tray in a private room, but it took no time to decide on the right one: a perfect, blue-white diamond, flanked by sapphires and set in white gold.

It was a classic, just like the woman who would wear it.

He put the little red box in his pocket, raced back to Saks and found Sage agonizing over the bowling-ball case, the sack and a lunchbox—at least, that's what they looked like to him.

"Where were you?" she whispered. "I wanted your opinion—"

"In the men's room," he said blithely, and told the clerk they'd take all three.

Caleb Wilde, world-class problem-solver.

"I keep telling you," Sage said, all bluster but with something indescribably tender in her eyes, "that you're impossible."

"I am," he said somberly...

And then a funny thing happened.

A lightning bolt came straight out of the ceiling.

It might as well have, because all at once and with unerring certainty, he knew he wasn't impossible at all.

He was simply a man head over heels in love.

CHAPTER TWELVE

CALEB poured himself a brandy, stood at the windows looking out at Central Park, and told himself to calm down.

Sage was in the bedroom.

He could see her whenever he turned around, surrounded by boxes and shopping bags and all the things he'd bought for her.

She was excited and happy.

He was excited and happy…and an absolute wreck.

The little red box was burning a hole in his pocket.

He brought the brandy snifter to his lips, took a slow, warming mouthful of the amber liquid.

Asking her to marry him had been easy. Well, more or less. Proposing had been a logical choice.

Telling a woman you loved her didn't have anything to do with logic.

It meant putting your heart on the line. And he'd never done anything remotely like it before.

The glass shook in his hand.

Amazing.

He'd faced capture by the enemy, torture, even death. But this—telling Sage he loved her…

What if she didn't love him? What if she said, *"That's very nice to hear, Caleb, and I like you, I like going to bed with you but…"*

Sage must have felt his eyes on her because she spun toward the door and when he saw the joy in her face, his heart lifted.

"You crazy man," she said, "buying me all this!"

"Just so you know," he said, straight-faced, "I have a no-returns policy."

She laughed. So did he. He put down the snifter, opened his arms and she flew into them. Her laughter turned to tears and when he asked why she was crying she said it was because she was so happy.

"Right," he said, gathering her closer, feeling her tears on his throat.

No wonder the idea of baring his soul to her scared the crap out of him.

That was why finding the right time, the right place to give her the ring and tell her he loved her was so important.

Women didn't operate on the same emotional plane as men. They were impossible to predict, impossible to comprehend, and, God, holding her like this was everything.

But it wasn't enough.

So he kissed her. Caressed her. Took her to bed.

And he knew it was crazy but he wanted to tell her he loved her when he could concentrate on finding the right words, and he couldn't concentrate on anything but this, this, when she was naked beneath him; this, when he was deep, so deep inside her...

By the time sanity returned, they were running late.

The concierge had snagged him last-minute dinner reservations at Daniel and front-row-center tickets for a play that had just opened to glowing reviews.

The restaurant was perfect, as always; the service impeccable, the meal itself elegant—but it wasn't the place to give her the ring and tell her he loved her because if he did, they'd never make it to the theater, and the entire evening, from start to finish, was all for her.

At the theater, while she watched the actors, Caleb watched

her, loving her total concentration, her absolute stillness. He reached for her hand, brought it to his lips and kissed her fingers.

"Hey," he said softly, at the end of the first act, and she gave him a private, tender smile that leached the fear right out of him.

She loved him.

He was certain of it.

All he had to do was get through the next couple of hours and then he could tell her what was in his heart.

At last, they were going home. Well, not "home" but to the penthouse suite that had become their own private world.

They rode the elevator in the best kind of silence, she with her head on his shoulder, he with his arm tightly around her waist. When they reached their door, Caleb opened it, then swung her up into his arms and elbowed the door shut behind him.

He was done with waiting.

It was time.

He kissed her. Set her down slowly on her feet...

And saw the blinking red light on the sitting-room telephone.

No, he told himself, dammit, no! He was not putting this off for another minute...

"There's a message," Sage said.

Caleb shook his head. "It's only a message if we listen to it."

She laughed. "A lovely thought, but don't you want to find out what it is?"

"No." He locked his hands at the base of her spine. She leaned back, raised her arms, draped them around his neck, hands linked at the nape. "I'm not interested in messages tonight. That's why I shut off my cell phone hours ago."

"Ah."

He ducked his head, nuzzled a silky strand of hair back from her throat. "Ah, what?"

"Ah, then maybe whoever's trying to reach you is really, *really* trying to reach you."

That stopped him.

Maybe she was right.

He hadn't even looked at his phone since the afternoon.

"Okay," he said, reluctantly. "I'll check."

"Five minutes," she said. "That's all you get."

He tugged her closer and kissed her.

"Two minutes is all I'll need."

She smiled. "I'm going to get undressed."

"Don't," he said with a wicked grin. "That's my job, remember?"

She blushed, laughed, kissed him again. He watched her walk into the bedroom. Then he reached for the phone and followed its automated directions.

Sage shook her hair loose and brushed it.

It was a little damp.

The rain, which had ended in late afternoon, had started again when they were a block from the hotel.

They'd walked back from the theater.

Caleb had started to flag a taxi. She'd stopped him.

"Let's walk," she'd said.

"It's a long walk, honey."

"I know. But I've always loved walking in the city."

He couldn't think of another woman who'd say such a thing about doing a couple of miles of pavement.

"Okay," he'd said, talking her hand. "Let's walk."

They had, taking it slow, pausing to peer into shop windows, talking, laughing, two people learning more and more about each other.

When the rain started, they were only a couple of blocks from the hotel. It came down lightly, more a soft mist than rain, and Sage had turned her face up to it and Caleb had kissed her.

Now, her hair was curling.

Worse.

It was becoming a wild tangle.

Should she use the dryer? Or would Caleb like it this way?

She thought of him coming into the bedroom. Taking her in his arms. Kissing her. Stripping her out of her dress, a shimmering column of pale peach silk, out of her bra and panties, leaving her only in spiked gold heels, her hair tumbling down her back.

The perfect end to what had been a perfect night.

The restaurant. The theater. But most of all, Caleb. Her lover. More than her lover.

The man she loved.

A little tremor of delight danced down her spine.

She'd felt him watching her tonight. Felt something different in his eyes. In his touch. He was so wonderful, so tender, so good to her that it seemed wrong, maybe even dangerous to want more.

But she did.

She wanted his love—and tonight there'd been times she'd felt—she'd felt as if he might feel some deeper emotion for her…

"Stop," she whispered.

Caleb liked being with her. He liked taking her to bed. He'd asked her to become his wife.

Those things were enough. And if someday a miracle happened…

"Dammit, no!"

His voice carried clearly from the sitting room. Sage looked at the door, which stood ajar.

"Caleb?" she said.

He didn't answer. She could still hear him talking but she

couldn't make out the words. His voice was low now, the tone urgent.

She walked slowly to the door and looked into the sitting room.

He was standing before the windows, the telephone at his ear. He was upset; she knew him well enough by now to read the signs. Head up. Spine even straighter than usual. Broad shoulders taut. Long, muscled legs apart.

A little smile curved her lips.

Her lover was the most beautiful man she'd ever known.

You weren't supposed to call a man beautiful but there was no other word to describe him. He was beautiful, inside and out.

If only her mother had lived to meet him. To see how wrong she'd been.

Not all men were selfish. Not all of them were liars.

Caleb wasn't.

He was good and kind, generous and honest, and she loved him, loved him, loved him…

"What?" he said, his voice harsh.

Sage frowned. He'd gone from upset to angry. She wondered if she should go to him, let him see that she was there for him…

"Goddammit," he growled, "Jake shouldn't have said anything to you. This is my business, not his."

Sage's frown deepened.

Maybe what she ought to do was shut the door. Give Caleb some privacy…

"Addison. Listen to me."

Addison. His sister-in-law. His law partner.

"No, I am not going to discuss this now. Because I'm not alone, dammit, that's why. Is that so hard to understand?"

Sage jumped back guiltily as Caleb turned from the window. She used the door as a shield but he hadn't seen her. He was too furious to see anything, she realized, as he began pacing through the room.

"Okay. I get it. Jake only told you because you asked him if he knew how you could reach me when I didn't return your calls, but—"

He cocked his head, listening to his sister-in-law, every now and then muttering a harsh curse under his breath.

"Are you done?" he finally said. "Good. Now listen, and listen well. This woman, Sage Dalton, this situation, isn't anyone's affair but mine."

Cold fingers danced along Sage's spine.

This woman? This situation?

"I'm dealing with it. That's all you need to know."

Dealing with it. Oh God, he was *dealing with*—

"Yes. I do see that. The legal ramifications as opposed to anything else. Well, of course. A paternity test. Right. After the child is born. That'll eliminate any possibility of later claims."

A whimper rose in Sage's throat. *Caleb,* she thought, *oh Caleb!*

"Goddammit," he snarled, "no, I have not married her!" He ran his hand through his hair. "Do I seem that much of a fool? I know what has to be done and when to do it."

Sage fell back, her hand clamped over her mouth. *Do not throw up,* she told herself fiercely. *You haven't done that in weeks and, dammit, you're not going to start again now!*

"I understand." His voice quieted. "Yeah, you're right. I shouldn't have left you in the dark. The personal issues are one thing but the legal implications… Look, can you deal with this? Good. Excellent. Draw up something. Make it clear that the child will be mine. Only mine."

Sage looked around, frantic. She'd left her handbag somewhere…

There it was. A tiny silk evening purse. Not that it really

was hers. Caleb had bought it for her. He'd bought everything she was wearing.

She wanted to tear it all off, fling it into the corner, but she had to hurry. She could hear the murmur of his voice, calmer now, steadier, and why wouldn't it be?

She had never been his lover, she had been his—his plaything. His toy. Sex and a baby, in one neat package, though he wasn't convinced about the baby, he'd require a paternity test first and then, once he knew the DNA matched, he'd demand sole custody of his child.

That, at least, would make her baby's life different from hers.

Her child wouldn't be raised by a single, bitter, poverty-stricken mother. Her child would be raised by a wealthy, arrogant, self-important father who'd hand him over to nurses and nannies…

The hell he would.

This was her baby. Nobody else's.

Caleb Wilde might be congratulating himself on a game well played but the game wasn't over yet.

"Addison," he said, "I have to go. I'll call you tomorrow, once I've—"

"Talk to her now," Sage said, as she stepped into the sitting room. "You'll have all the time you need, I promise."

She knew she would always remember the look on Caleb's face. The dropped jaw, the open mouth, the stunned expression on his deceptively beautiful face.

"Sage?" he said. "Honey?"

She wanted to tell him what he could do with all those *honeys* and *sweethearts,* but it might take too long.

Instead, she flung open the door.

"Goodbye, Caleb."

"Sage! What the hell are you—"

The door slammed shut.

Caleb stared at it while he tried to figure out what was happening.

Addison was still talking, but who gave a damn?

"She's leaving me," Caleb said. "Sage is—"

He dropped the phone, ran for the door, pulled it open...

Too late.

The carpeted hall seemed to stretch into infinity.

And Sage was gone.

CHAPTER THIRTEEN

CALEB reached the elevators in time to see one going up and the other going down.

He ran for the fire stairs, took them two at a time, burst through the doors into the lobby...

Too late.

There was no one there except the clerks at the reception desk, who stared at him.

He knew how he must look.

Hair on end. A wild look in his eyes, as if the world had just ended.

The doorman saw him coming. It was a new guy, one Caleb had never seen before, and though he smiled politely, his eyes were full of caution.

"Sir? May I help you?"

"Did a woman just come through here?"

"Sir?"

"A woman," Caleb said impatiently. "My..." His what? What did he call her? What was she? Not his wife. His girlfriend? His fiancée? Dammit, none of those was right. "Blonde. Tall. She came in with me a little while ago."

"Oh. Yes, sir, she did. I offered to get a taxi for her but—"

Hell. Caleb looked through the glass doors. It wasn't just raining, it was pouring.

"Where did she go?"

"That way. Toward the corner of—"

Caleb took off, running.

He was in good shape. He always had been. He'd ridden horses since he was a kid; in high school and college, he'd played football. He'd completed the requisite twelve weeks of Marine Corps training before joining The Agency—he could still do a hundred push-ups, run a four-minute mile, no sweat.

He was grateful for it now because the rain was heavy, the wind had come up...

And, dammit, Sage was nowhere in sight.

Maybe the doorman had it wrong.

Maybe he was heading in the wrong direction—except, this was the way to the nearest subway stop and only his Sage would be pig-headed enough to ride the subway, alone, at this hour of the—

There she was.

The rain and wind made vision difficult but how many other women would be hightailing it along the street in a thin dress and skinny heels on a night like this?

Didn't she know enough, at least, to take off those shoes? If she slipped on the wet sidewalk and went down...

Caleb was already running at full speed.

Somehow, he ran harder.

Half a block away, he did something amazingly stupid.

He shouted her name.

She glanced back, and went from walking fast to running.

Great.

"Sage, goddammit," he shouted and his heart jumped straight into his throat because she was approaching the corner, not slowing down, another couple of inches and she'd be stepping off the curb...

A big-ass delivery truck was hurtling into the intersection.

"Sage," Caleb yelled, and on one final burst of speed he

wouldn't have imagined possible, he reached her, closed his arms around her and dragged her back against him.

For a heartbeat, they remained just that way, him holding her, she wrapped safely in his arms.

A wave of water big enough to have swamped the *Titanic* billowed over them.

"Dammit, dammit, dammit," Caleb snarled, and then he spun Sage around, saw her face awash with a mix of rain and tears, and he cursed again and kissed her.

Her lips clung to his just long enough to give him hope. Then she jerked back in his arms, slammed her fists against his shoulders and called him a name that might have made him laugh if his heart wasn't trying to claw its way out of his chest.

So, instead, he grabbed her wrists, pinned her hands between them, and took refuge in anger.

"What the hell were you thinking? Didn't you see the red light? Didn't you see that frigging truck? Another couple of seconds and you might have—you might have—" The rush of words stopped; the enormity of what had almost happened shot through him, left him shaken. "I almost lost you," he whispered.

"As if it matters," she said, her voice trembling.

"What are you talking about?"

"Or maybe it does. Maybe you really do want your child—"

Her teeth started to chatter. Caleb yanked off his suit jacket and wrapped it around her.

"I don't want anything from—"

"Taxi," he yelled, as a cab approached, but it shot by.

"Caleb. Do you hear me? I said, I don't want—"

"Taxi!"

The second cab shot by, too. It was New-York-in-the-Rain, when taxi drivers suddenly went blind.

Okay.

No taxi. And no cell phone. He'd left it in their suite…but, hallelujah, there was a coffee shop a few feet away.

"Come on," he said, tightening his arm around her.

She shook her head, dug in her heels, refused to move.

"Sage. Come on."

"No."

"Sweetheart. We're going to drown out here."

"I'm not your sweetheart. And I'm not going anywhere with you."

"Of course you're going with me. Where else would you go?"

"Back to Brooklyn. Back to my life. Away from you and your—your lies."

Caleb grasped her shoulders. Even in her soaked, still-sexy heels, she was inches shorter than he; he drew her to her toes until their faces were level.

"I have never lied to you!"

"You damn well did!"

"When? What did I say that wasn't true?"

"You said—you said you—you wanted us to be a family. You. Me. Our baby."

"That was—that *is*—the absolute truth!"

"You said—you said you cared for me…"

"Yeah." His voice roughened. "That one was a lie."

She started to turn away but he framed her face between his hands, locked his eyes on hers and thought, fleetingly, that he was about to make the most important declaration of his life to the most important person in his life while they both courted pneumonia.

So much for planning, logic and the right time and place.

"It was the biggest lie of my life because I don't 'care' for you, sweetheart, I love you. I adore you. With everything I

am, everything I ever will be. And if you were to leave me…
if you were to leave me…"

She stared at him. Her mouth trembled. Hell, all of her was
trembling. Caleb put his arm around her, drew her close and
led her toward the coffee shop.

"I'm not going in there," Sage said, but without conviction.

Caleb opened the door. "Heck," he said with a quick smile,
"here's that opportunity you were so hot for, remember? The
chance to discuss the intimate details of our lives and, if we're
really lucky, get some input from a waitress."

She looked up at him.

Then she laughed.

It was quick, over almost before it began, but it was the
first positive thing that had happened since she'd run away

Still, he was afraid to make too much of it because something was definitely wrong, very wrong, and if she told him
that she didn't feel about him the way he felt about her—

"Caleb."

Her whisper made him blink. And brought him back to
reality.

There were people in the place. A couple of guys at the
counter, beefy hands wrapped around big mugs of steaming
coffee. Two couples in one of the booths, hamburgers and
fries in front of them. There was a counterman in a stained
white apron, a waitress in a pink-and-white uniform…

And they were all staring at Sage. At him. At what probably looked like a pair of half-drowned idiots, dripping water
on the scuffed, none-too-clean tile floor.

Caleb cleared his throat.

"Hi," he said brightly, and sent a smile in the waitress's
direction. "Okay to, ah, to take a booth?"

She shrugged. "I guess."

"And, uh, and could we have a big stack of napkins? So
we can dry off."

Another shrug. Caleb led Sage to a booth. She slid in on one side. He slid in on the other.

"Coffee?"

"Please. Actually, make it one coffee. And one herbal tea. My wife can't drink coffee. She's pregnant."

Sage blushed. "I'm not," she said quickly. "His wife, I mean."

"But she's pregnant," he said, and her blush deepened.

Hell, what was the matter with him? Stuff was just falling out of his mouth...

Stuff was just falling out of his mouth...

"Oh, hell," he said softly.

Because all at once, he knew exactly why the woman he loved had left him.

"You heard that phone call," he said.

"What phone call?"

She said it casually, with a lift of the shoulders, but he wasn't buying it.

She'd heard him talking with Addison, and when he thought back on it, he understood that every terse, angry thing he'd said could easily have sounded like an indictment.

"Sage. Honey—"

"Napkins," the waitress said, dumping a stack six inches high on the table.

Caleb nodded. "Thanks."

"And your coffee. And that herbal tea... Here it is. Hope orange spice is okay."

"It's fine."

"I thought we might have lemon verbena, but—"

"What you brought is perfect."

The waitress eyed him narrowly. Then she went back to the counter, and Caleb leaned across the table.

"You know what phone call," he said. "The one I made to Addison."

"Your sister-in-law. Your law partner." Sage's voice shook. "The woman who's drawing up the papers you think I'm going to sign that will give you custody of my baby."

"Our baby. And no, I don't want custody. Why would I, when he'll be our child?"

"She. It might be a she."

"I don't give a damn about sex!"

"You most certainly do give a damn about sex! That's the only reason you—you want me around."

Someone laughed.

Caleb shot a furious glare around the room. Then he looked at Sage.

"I love you," he said fiercely. "Do you hear me, dammit? I. Love. You!"

"You don't. And you said you believed me when I told you the baby was yours but—but that was just another lie!"

Caleb grabbed her hand, wouldn't let her tug it free.

"You heard me tell Addison we'll want a paternity test after the baby's born."

Sage nodded. She didn't trust herself to speak. It wasn't easy, letting him see only her anger and not her sorrow.

She'd loved Caleb with all her heart.

Even worse, she still loved him, liar that he was.

"Sage." His hand tightened on hers. "The test is to get David's father off our backs, once and for all."

"No. He can't still think—"

"It's partly my fault. I'm supposed to be one hell of an attorney but I got so caught up in us that I forget to contact him. He reached Addison and told her he won't accept the truth without proof."

"Oh, Caleb—"

"I know. I made a huge mistake."

Sage could feel the pain lifting from her heart, but Caleb had one last thing to explain.

"And—and I heard what you told her about the wedding. That you weren't crazy, that no, you hadn't married me…"

"Right." Caleb looked at the ceiling, as if he might find help there, but all he saw was an old-fashioned, slowly revolving fan. "Addison thought we might have eloped. I have to admit, the thought occurred to me. I mean, there's not a man alive wants to put on a monkey suit…" He shook his head. "But I'm not a complete fool. My sisters, probably Addison, too, would skin me alive if we denied them all that stuff. The music. The flowers. You in a long white gown, me all gussied up…"

Sage was staring at him. He couldn't read anything in her eyes.

"Honey," he said gruffly, "I know I've made a lot of mistakes. The biggest one was not telling you how much I love you right away. See, I wanted the perfect time and place."

"Like we have now," Sage said, and—*Thank you, God*—she was smiling.

"Sage. Tell me you love me, too. Tell me that I wasn't imagining what I saw in your eyes, tasted in your kisses."

"I love you," Sage said quietly.

"Or tell me there's at least a chance you'll come to—" Caleb blinked. "You love me?"

"Of course." She smiled through her tears. "I'll always love you, Sir Knight."

Caleb got to his feet. Went to her side of the booth, dug in his pocket and dropped to his knees, right on that wet, messy floor.

"Sage," he said.

She caught her breath. There was a little red box in his hand.

"Honey." Caleb opened the box. The fire of a thousand suns flashed inside it. "Will you marry me? For the only reason that matters, sweetheart. For love."

Sage laughed. She cried. She bent down to him, clasped his face, pressed her lips to his.

"What she means," the waitress said, "is yes."

Caleb rose to his feet and drew Sage up and into his arms.

The waitress was holding their check and smiling; her eyes—eyes that had surely seen everything the city could offer—glinted with suspicious dampness.

Gently, Caleb took the check from her hand and put it on the table. Then he took a handful of bills from his pocket, clasped her hand and folded her fingers around them.

"Thank you," he said.

She gaped at the bills. Then she ran after them as they headed for the door.

"Wait," she said. "Mister! This is way, way too much for—"

Caleb turned toward her.

"If I hadn't been such a fool, if we'd gone into a coffee shop right away and asked someone just like you for advice…" He cleared his throat. "Trust me," he said huskily. "It isn't anywhere near enough."

The rain had stopped. It was night, impossible for there to be a rainbow, but under the streetlights, Sage's engagement ring cast a rainbow of its own.

The very first taxi they saw stopped to pick them up.

When they reached their suite. Caleb kissed Sage, then said, "One last thing." He held her hand while he hit a button on his cell phone. "Addison? It's Caleb. I need a favor. Get Jake in the room. He is? Travis, too? Great. Okay, put us on speaker phone." *Speaker phone,* Caleb thought with a quick laugh, *his new best friend.* "I have some news—and then, if one of you would call Em and Jaimie and Lissa…" He listened, shook his head in happy disbelief. "Perfect," he told Sage. "My sisters, even the General are there, for the weekend."

"Caleb," Sage whispered, "what are you doing?"

He kissed her. "Here we go, honey," he said, and took one last deep breath. "Everybody? I'm coming home. With the woman I love. And, guys? We're pregnant."

There was a second of surprised silence. Then, cheers and applause sounded tinnily through the phone.

But Caleb and Sage weren't listening.

She was weeping, he was smiling, and they were wrapped in each other's arms.

* * * * *

A sneaky peek at next month...

MODERN™

INTERNATIONAL AFFAIRS, SEDUCTION & PASSION GUARANTEED

My wish list for next month's titles...

In stores from 21st December 2012:

❏ Beholden to the Throne – Carol Marinelli

❏ Her Little White Lie – Maisey Yates

❏ The Incorrigible Playboy – Emma Darcy

❏ The Enigmatic Greek – Catherine George

In stores from 4th January 2013:

❏ The Petrelli Heir – Kim Lawrence

❏ Her Shameful Secret – Susanna Carr

❏ No Longer Forbidden? – Dani Collins

❏ The Night That Started It All – Anna Cleary

❏ The Secret Wedding Dress – Ally Blake

Available at WHSmith, Tesco, Asda, Eason, Amazon and Apple

Just can't wait?

Special Offers

Every month we put together collections and longer reads written by your favourite authors.

Here are some of next month's highlights— and don't miss our fabulous discount online!

On sale 21st December

On sale 4th January

On sale 4th January

Save 20% on all Special Releases